EAGLE EYE

DARCY FLYNN

Jacque,
Best,
Darcy
Flynn

ACKNOWLEDGMENTS

I want to thank my readers and fans of *Keeper of My Heart* for insisting I write Jill's story. I have to say, I had so much fun linking a character from my first book with *Eagle Eye,* Book 2 in my Like No Other Series.

I know, I told you book two would be Ethan and Amanda's story, but after much nagging from Jill and her undercover journalist, I caved. Ethan and Amanda's story is coming, I promise.

To my editor, Ally Robertson, as always, your insightful critique has made my story better. Thank you. To my creative team, Rae Monet for her cover design, Karen Duvall for creating the flat, and Jesse Gordon, my formatter. Thank you.

To my lovely critique partners, Cindy Brannam and Jeanne Hardt, I so appreciate your timely suggestions and most of all your friendship. And many thanks to my cousin, Glenda Beall, for agreeing to beta-read for me at the last minute. Thanks for your helpful input.

Finally, I wish to thank my niece, Elizabeth Austin, a New Yorker, for answering all of my questions regarding New York City.

One morning a couple of years ago, I was at Hugo's Restaurant in West Hollywood having breakfast. I sat outside at a small table for two. A couple seated at the small bistro table next to me had recently left and the waitress hadn't yet picked up their plates.

A handsome young man, dressed in loose clothing, with wavy longish hair and a short beard walked by at a nice clip. He briefly stopped at their table and grabbed a napkin. To my astonishment, without missing a beat, he lifted a spoon, scraped the last bit of food onto the napkin, then shoveled it into his mouth as he continued walking. He acted without the least hesitation. Without thought. As if he'd done this many times before.

I sat stunned. Horrified at what had transpired, I watched him walk the length of the restaurant, then turn right before he disappeared.

When the homeless young man strode off, my heart cried out to stop him, to offer him a meal. But what 60-year-old woman runs after a thirty-year-old homeless guy? So, I did the normal, *sane* thing, simply sat there and watched him leave. I glanced around at those seated near me and not one of them seemed to have noticed him.

I've thought about that young man many times since then, re-playing the scene over and over in my head. In my daydream, I call out to him. He stops and turns. I offer to buy him breakfast, and although surprised, he accepts. We sit at the bistro table on a beautiful California morning and I discover more about him over a hearty breakfast.

But, that's not how it happened.

I thought about those who loved this young man, who worried about him. And mostly, I thought about his mother. As I pondered this man's condition I played several scenarios in my head. Maybe he was a spy, undercover, and fleeing his most recent captors. Nearly starved. Why else would he eat off the plate of a stranger?

I knew someday I'd give him a story and a reason to do what he did. Thus my undercover journalist hero was born. Then I gave my heroine the heart I'd wished I'd had that day. The heart that was in me, but afraid to act. I gave her the courage to actually go after the homeless man and the will to at least try and change his life.

Every once in a while there is a reader who's so much more than a reader, she's a fan...

Leslee Willmore, middle school librarian extraordinaire, thanks for loving my stories! This one's for you!

CHAPTER ONE

Jill Jeffrey waited near the entrance to New York City's *Plaza Hotel* hat and coat-check station. The hum of activity from tonight's charity auction filtered down the hallway from the ball-room.

She casually folded her arms and watched Mark Billings shrug into his overcoat. Two months ago, Mark had dropped her, Jill Jeffrey of JJ Designs, and she still smarted from the insult. When he'd discovered she wasn't one of the *Jeffreys of Scarsdale*, but instead a Jeffrey from some obscure Maryland fishing village, he'd lost interest and ended their relationship. In hindsight, he'd made her feel inadequate and out of her element on more than one occasion. That should have been a clue to the real Mark.

"Leaving so soon?" she asked.

Mark paused, his coat barely over his shoulders, and glanced back at her.

"Sorry, but I've had my fill of charity functions for one night. And, I wasn't about to sit one minute longer listening to you and Eleanor bicker over some silly fashion nonsense."

"Exactly."

"What's that supposed to mean?" He secured the last button.

Mark was prone to making frivolous bets. She'd succumbed to one or two of his herself, so a suitable payback had been in order.

"Remember when you told me you'd gladly *pay* to see Eleanor Watts and me argue over the latest color trends in fashion?" Folding her arms, she raised a brow daring him to deny it.

"That's because Eleanor is an obnoxious know-it-all." He shrugged, smiling. "I thought it might be humorous to see you two go at it." His smile suddenly faded. "Wait a minute. Are you telling me that entire scene was a set up?"

"It was."

Huffing out a breath, he eyed her critically. "You not only dress like a fifteen-year-old, but you act like one. I don't get it. With your talent, you could be designing for New York City's A-List. But in that *get up* you look like some over-made-up, under-sexed teenage girl."

Jill sucked in air. "This *get up* is for charity and one of my hottest designs."

Shaking his head, he walked away and it was all her short legs could do to keep up with him. When he pushed through the hotel doors onto Fifth Avenue, she finally caught up with him and only because he stopped at the hotel's taxi stand.

"Hey, we're not through here. Don't even think about leaving until you pay up." Palm up, she wiggled her fingers. "Come on, Mark, it was your bet and this is for charity. It's not like you can't afford it." She angled her head to the side and gleefully watched as he reached into his pants pocket. "And I promise, your donation is safe with me."

"Donation?" He clamped his jaw together. "More like larceny." He shoved four crisp one hundred dollar bills into her palm. "Now that you've made your fortune, I'm surprised you still feel the need to resort to such childish trickery."

"And spoil all the fun? Besides, my fortune is hardly visible compared to yours." Her income at this point in her career was far from fortune status. Everything she'd made went back into her company. She'd eaten enough ramen noodles to last a lifetime and if she didn't hit it big, and soon, she'd turn into one. The rent in the fashion district was steep, as well as all of her other expenses. One needed deep pockets to live in Manhattan, but it was the place to be if she wanted to be successful in the fashion world.

"Tonight we're here to raise money for several good causes. No bet is off limits."

"All right." He scanned the surrounding area. "If that's the case, I dare you to try one of your schemes with, let's say…that guy over there." He pointed to a man on the corner who was holding a sign that read, 'Homeless Will Work for Food.'

Hunkered down into his jacket, the man shuffled from one foot to the other, most likely to keep warm.

"That's low. Even for you."

"I'm not talking about taking his money, but something else."

"Which is…"

"Get him to go out with you." He gave her the once-over. "Dressed like that."

She placed her fists meaningfully on her hips. Admittedly, a gesture which never intimidated him… Or, anyone else for that matter. But there was something about fists-on-hips that made her feel taller.

"And wake up with my throat slit in the morning?"

"It doesn't have to be a *date-date*." He paused for a moment, then his eyes lit up. "I know. Just get him to go back to the hotel ballroom with you for a little while—let's say for an hour. That shouldn't be too difficult for you. I mean, look at the guy. He's shivering in his shoes, and by the looks of him, could use a hot meal."

"And how do you suggest I do that?"

"The same way you treated me mere minutes ago. Con the guy."

"Oh, please." She rolled her eyes. "Be serious for a change."

"Turn on the charm. You're so good at that."

She studied the man on the corner. Except for his age, he reminded her of Steve from the soup kitchen. Same wire-rimmed eyeglasses, scruffy beard, and hair in desperate need of a trim.

A familiar ache rose in her heart. She could never imagine being homeless. Even if she'd had no success, she knew too many people who'd help her. She wondered who this man was and why he didn't have at least one someone to come to his aid. Surely everybody had somebody.

She shook her head and fixed her gaze on Mark. "You arrogant, son of a gun."

He'd taken on that smug expression she used to think was classy and sophisticated. How could she ever have mistaken that self-satisfied, superior smirk for anything other than arrogance?

"What makes you think I'd even contemplate using that poor man for your personal entertainment?"

"Because, I'll donate ten-thousand dollars to any cause you want."

Her heart stopped, then thudded in a mad rush inside her chest. Any cause? She thought of Like No Other and the *real* good an amount like that could do for Annie's girls. Not to mention the possible position on Annie's board of directors, if she could raise such a sum. Such a position would give her an added respect in the fashion community. A leg up. The clout needed. She'd never dreamed it could be handed to her so easily and by Mark of all people. But, then again, he would know.

A momentary twinge of guilt nagged. When did charity work become all about what she'd wanted? Appalled at the way her thoughts were going, she quickly pushed them away. Before she could think of how to respond, Mark continued.

"Oh, and the hour can't be you just standing there on the corner with him. You have to get him inside. Eat. Dance. You know the drill."

"Dance?"

"For crying out loud, Jill. It's a figure of speech. You don't actually have to dance with the man."

Well, in that case... Dollar signs danced before her eyes, negating the rising stab of guilt at the thought of using the poor man in a wager. She gnawed her bottom lip and glanced again at the shabbily dressed stranger only a few yards away.

His height alone intimidated, giving her second thoughts. But he'd never have to *know* he was being used. Plus, it *was* for a good cause. Her mind argued as her gaze lingered. She'd offer him a hot meal. Get him off the street and out of the cold. What could be so wrong with that?

"Look at the guy." Mark pressed his lips together in irritation. "He's freezing out here. Come on. He'll thank you for it."

Mark spoke as if he'd been reading her thoughts.

"Do you think he really wants to stand on a street corner in these temps begging for food, if he doesn't have to?" Mark's deep voice cajoled, coaxing her with the visual picture of this street person comfortably seated eating a hot meal.

Admittedly, the thought of what the charity could do with that kind of money almost made her giddy. She'd hoped her auction items would bring a couple of thousand dollars at tonight's Pick Your Charity Event, which included the Like No Other Foundation. But to have four or five times that amount handed to her for one little hour with the man on the corner was too appealing to turn down. She had no idea how she'd manage it, but she had to convince him to spend the next hour with her.

"Any cause I want?"

"That's what I said."

"This could really go a long way to help Like No Other."

"Seriously?"

"Yes, it's the annual Pick Your Charity and I pick them."

"Who in their right mind would donate to LNO, especially since the Alex Langdon thing."

"My point exactly. LNO needs this money. Donations have been down." She gnawed her inner lip and eyed the homeless stranger on the corner. "Okay. I'll do it. But. . .you'll pay twenty thousand."

Mark blanched and eyed her as if she'd lost her mind.

"You heard me. I'll do it for twenty thousand dollars. You can have your kicks, Mr. Nobody on the corner will have a hot meal, and Annie's girls will benefit."

"And you, won't you benefit?" He cocked a brow at her. "As I recall, such a sum would help you garner a most coveted position on her board of directors."

Heat crept up her cheeks, not even the sting of cold air could quench. Too much to hope Mark hadn't noticed, but his ready-smirk told her otherwise.

"Teenage girls are my bread and butter. Of course I want to help them and being on Annie's board will give me more access to do just that."

"And more standing in our fair community," he said.

"You can keep your *standing*. You have enough for ten people." She knew that wasn't completely true. Standing was everything in her line of business. In her few short years here, she'd learned connections and money were everything. Unfortunately, who you knew and not your talent garnered the most respect. The insanely successful arrived through someone of status, no matter what line of work they pursued.

"You drive a hard bargain, Jill." Chuckling, he pulled out his pen and check book. "You do know I would've given you more."

"Yes, and I'm sure I'll have another opportunity to secure more donations from you in the future."

He handed her the check. "You almost make me sorry we stopped dating." He shrugged. "I always did love your sassy side."

"As I recall, it was my sass you despised." *And my social status even more.*

He shrugged again. "True. You do have a tendency to go overboard at times."

Jill glanced at the check. "You need to make this out to Like No Other, not to me."

"Don't worry." He slid the check book and pen inside his Dolce & Gabbana suit jacket. "I trust you to get it to the right people."

She nodded, then clamped her right hand on the collar of his overcoat and pulled.

"Hey. What are doing?"

"Take it off."

"Like hell, I will. It's below freezing."

"You will and right now. I have to have some segue with the man and what better than a warm coat."

"It's cashmere for God's sake."

"And, you can buy ten more."

Jill helped Mark shrug out of the overcoat just as his taxi arrived. He wrapped his arms around his torso and climbed into the yellow vehicle. "Don't bother getting that back to me. There's no telling where that guy's been."

Folding the coat over her arm, she watched the red taillights of Mark's taxi blend in with the traffic.

Any other time, she would have laughed off Mark's insults and crazy suggestions. Not that anything about this situation was funny. Truthfully, she was a bit nervous.

She glanced around the area. It was well lit and people were milling about, and the patrol car parked down the street was definitely a plus. No reason not to feel safe. All she had to do was get the man back inside the hotel, spend an hour in his company, and introduce him to some of her friends so Mark would know she'd fulfilled her side of the bargain.

Easy.

She turned toward her unsuspecting victim, hugged Mark's coat to her chest and focused on the man's face. His scruffy beard couldn't hide his masculine jaw, or his firm lips. On closer inspection, he was much younger than she'd first thought. Possibly late twenties, or early thirties. No more than that.

Compassion tugged at her heart. She'd been so blessed. Her middle class upbringing in Paige Point, Maryland had been idyllic. A happy childhood, loving parents and a younger brother who adored her. Even though her line of clothes had done fairly well, her family was the real wealth.

The man hunched his shoulders as if that small movement could keep out the cold. How does a person get here? She continued to assess him. His pants fit a bit loose, but she could tell they were expensive. He'd probably gotten them from a second-hand store. You could get a lot of high-end threads at places like that. Either that or he'd just recently fallen on hard times. There was an army-green backpack at his feet.

In that moment, he leaned toward the car that had stopped next to him and took what looked like cash from the driver. He nodded his thanks as the light turned green and the car pulled away.

Green meant go, so she may as well get on with it. She sucked in a deep 'can do' breath and walked with purpose toward him.

* * *

Cameron Phillips hunched his shoulders against the cold wishing he'd had more than yesterday's newspaper lining his jacket. One of several tricks he'd learned from Eddie, who lived under the overpass in a makeshift lean-to next to his.

Like Eddie, he made his from cardboard boxes he'd scavenged from nearby trash bins. The best boxes came from local appliance stores. The bigger, the better. And if you timed it right, you might find a doublewide refrigerator-size before the store broke it down for recycling.

He shivered and clenched his jaw to keep his teeth from chattering.

"Excuse me."

Cam swiveled and gazed into the upturned face of a teenage girl. Her hesitant brown eyes held a hint of boldness as she stared up at him. The tip of her nose glowed pink from the cold. She was dressed in brightly colored leggings, an oversized hot pink sweater, and a felt hat of the same color. A multi-colored scarf hung loosely around her neck and she was hugging a bundle of something soft against her chest.

Good Lord.

"Get lost kid. You shouldn't be here." He turned away, hoping she'd get the message, but not before her young fawn eyes widened in surprise.

"Oh, I get that all the time," she said.

Curious, he glanced back over his shoulder. She flashed an engaging smile, which further exposed the bold twinkle in her gaze. Any hesitancy he thought he'd noticed earlier had quickly faded with her bright, welcoming, smile.

"Excuse me?" he said.

"You see, I'm a fashion designer. Teen girls are my specialty." She beamed up at him as if that explained everything, and held out what he now realized was a man's overcoat.

"Please take it. It's awfully cold." Her smile broadened. "No strings, I promise."

Eyeing the cashmere coat, he cupped his hands to his mouth and blew. His warm breath took the sting of cold from his palms, but only for a second.

"I didn't steal it, if that's what's worrying you," she said.

"No—" At that moment an NYPD blue and white cruised by catching his attention. "But someone may think I did."

She glanced around. "Like who?"

"That cop for one." He nodded in the direction of a New York policeman sitting astride a horse on the opposite corner. "I'm not sure he'd take too kindly to me talking to an underage female, either."

"Look, I'm old enough to vote *and* drink if that makes you feel any better."

It didn't.

He eyed the coat in her arms. His ears, nose, and fingers were already numb. "Okay, if you're sure."

"I'm sure."

Her soft laugh was as sparkling as her smile, but he still wasn't convinced she wasn't under age.

He glanced at the cop. "First, show me your driver's license."

She stopped smiling, but her eyes held merriment as she complied with his request.

She slipped the document from her sparkly shoulder bag and handed it to him. After adjusting his gold-rimmed eyeglasses on his nose, he studied the information.

"Jillian Marie Jeffrey. Five feet, two inches tall. Brown eyes and hair." He gazed at her, surprised at how serious she'd become. Gone was the glittering smile and twinkling eyes. All *telling* signs the license *was* fake. But, sure. He'd play along. "I see that you are indeed… Old. Enough."

He handed the license back and took the coat. He quickly pushed his arms through the expensive fabric, stifling a sigh as his shivering limbs relaxed into the warmth it provided.

"Thank you. Now you really should go. You may be of age, but you still look fifteen. That cop has been eyeing us ever since you walked up. I don't want any trouble."

"You know," she said, ignoring him. "I couldn't help see that your sign says you're hungry."

He stared at her, wondering if she were that dense or simply up to something. "Look. Thank you for the coat. But you need to get out of here."

What young woman acts like this? Not a normal one.

She raised her chin, which added about an inch to her small stature and eyed him like Sister Mary Margaret from St Patrick's Middle School. He shivered, and it wasn't from the cold.

"You aren't going to leave are you?" he said.

An impish grin spread across her face. She clamped her bottom lip with her teeth and slowly shook her head.

He glanced around the area, then back at her. "Look. If this is some kind of reality show, where you make sport of the street person, I'm not interested."

"G-Good heavens." She blinked and licked her hot pink lips. "You *are* suspicious. But, I'm surprised you're not more curious. Unless, this…" She waved her hand between the two of them. "…is an everyday occurrence for you."

"Hardly."

This girl was something else.

"Okay, here's the truth." She gave him a wide-eyed Bambi look. "I'm participating in a fundraiser, scavenger hunt thing, and have to bring a stranger back to the hotel ballroom. I'm so close to winning. More importantly, I *have* to beat my ex-boyfriend."

The wealthy and their games. He really had no time for this…

For a brief moment her smile faltered, then she folded her pink, sweater-covered arms across her chest, and gazed up at him with the most engaging gleam in her eyes. Eyes that held a hint of appeal mingled with audacious charm, which he found irresistible. He had a sudden image of all the young men she probably had lined up at her beck and call.

"Look. This isn't rocket science," she said. "I'm offering you a hot meal in a warm place. Just for an hour, in that hotel, right behind us. You help me. I help you. What do you say?"

"A good deed and all of that?" he asked.

She faltered, glanced at her feet, then back up at him. "Something like that. And...because you remind me of someone." She added with a tentative smile.

In spite of her seemingly forthright innocence, this girl was hiding something. Now he *was* curious. A beautiful young woman, obviously well-off, hands him one of the most expensive coats one can buy, then offers him the warmth of the hotel and a hot meal.

Scavenger hunt, my ass. Damned right he was curious. He wondered again if her ID could be phony, but decided to ignore it.

"A place like The Plaza may not want the likes of me in their glamorous hotel," he said.

"Not to worry." She flitted her right hand in the air. "You'll be with me."

"Do you always get your way?"

"Of course." Her uncertainty from earlier vanished as a confident expression formed on her pretty face.

He swept his arm in the direction of the hotel. "After you, fashion designer, Jillian Marie Jeffrey."

CHAPTER TWO

Cam bowed slightly and couldn't help but notice the soft pink infusing Jill's cheeks. Barely visible under the city lights, but it was most certainly there.

Neither spoke as they walked into The Plaza's Terrace Room. They weaved through the white cloth-covered tables, the crystal, fine china, and low burning candles. She finally motioned him to a vacant table near the center of the ornate ballroom and to a seat that still had an untouched salad plate. He lowered his backpack onto the chair next to him and sat down.

"So this is how the other half lives."

She flagged a waiter and ordered dinner for him and hot coffee for them both.

"Looks like dinner is over," he said. "Are you sure this is okay?"

"It's fine." She shifted in her chair and glanced left. "Most everyone has gathered at the auction tables."

"Making it a good time to bring in the beggar from the street. Is that it?"

Her face fell and she licked her pink lips. "No. Of course not."

"Sorry. Forgive my sarcasm, but you'd be surprised how people like me are treated on a daily basis. Used. Discarded. It's hard not to be cynical or suspicious."

She lowered her gaze to his salad plate. Had he hit a nerve?

"So, who is this person I remind you of?"

"A very nice man named Steve."

"Steve, huh?"

She nodded.

"And how do you know I'm nice?"

"Well, I guess that remains to be seen."

"Did Steve live on the street, too?"

She lifted her gaze to his. "Yes."

"And did you offer him a hot meal?"

"I did."

"Nice."

The greens had wilted slightly and he was thankful the server chose that moment to bring the main course. Roast beef, new potatoes, and asparagus.

"This looks good." He nodded to the plate in front of him and dove in. "I hate to eat in front of a lady, but…"

"Oh, please. Go ahead." She quickly perused the room, then gave him her full attention. "I hope it doesn't make you nervous when people watch you eat."

"No, not at all."

"So. What's your name?"

"Phil."

"What do you do? Or should I say, what *did* you do?"

"I'm an artist." He scooped a spoonful of salad dressing onto the wilted lettuce, then stabbed a clump with his fork.

"Oh, my best friend is an artist. Katie…or Catherine Clare as she's known in the art world. She paints the most amazing land-scapes." Jill wrapped her fingers around her coffee cup and took a sip. "One of her paintings is in this hotel. Maybe you've heard of her?"

"Sorry, I haven't. When you're on the streets you lose contact with those who are successful in the world."

"So, you're a starving artist."

He froze, fork midway in the air and stared at her. "At the moment, it does seem like it."

"Oh, my gosh. I…I can't believe I said that." She raised a hand to her heart. Remorse filled her golden-brown eyes. "I'm such an idiot."

"Nonsense." He shrugged. "You spoke the truth. Don't worry about it."

"It's just…you seem awfully young to be impoverished."

"Age has nothing to do with poverty. But, from the looks of you, I guess I shouldn't expect you to know that."

"What do you mean, exactly?"

He swallowed, then took a sip of water. "You're obviously well-off. I'm sure it's safe to say you've never lacked for anything. Am I right?"

"Technically, that's true. My needs have always been met."

She smiled sweetly and the hint of a dimple appeared on her right cheek. He hadn't noticed it when they were outside.

Propping her elbows on the table, she rested her chin in her hands. "Maybe I should make you my protégée."

Was she serious? Her gaze was innocent enough, but he'd met people like her before - offering false hope just to make a point.

"Maybe." He shrugged and cut through the asparagus. "How successful are you?"

She chuckled. "I'm getting there."

"Enough to pay my way?"

"Well…" She caught her bottom lip with her teeth, picked up his hand from the table and inspected it. A tiny frown crossed her creamy complexion. She was quite beautiful. The vibrant colors she wore suited her deep caramel eyes.

"What kind of art do you do?" she asked.

"Photography. And, I write."

She released his fingers, then folded her hands primly in front of her.

"Anything I would've read?"

"Depends. Do you read the Tabloids?"

Her lovely eyes briefly widened, then narrowed as if confused. "No, I don't."

Her face clouded over and the sudden interest in her teaspoon didn't go unnoticed. He'd disappointed her. Why would it matter? What was he to her, anyway?

Then it hit him. She was a do-gooder. First it was this Steve guy and now he, Lord bless him, was her latest project. She continued to fiddle with a spoon, refusing to look at him.

So Jillian was definitely more than just a pretty face. She had a conscience. Morals. He could see her mind working—wondering. Had he lain in wait outside celebrity homes hoping to catch a glimpse? Had he shown up unwanted at funerals of the rich and famous? She tapped her finger near her mouth and lifted her gaze to search the room. No doubt, already regretting her attempt at intervention.

"Looking for someone?" he asked.

Her gaze fluttered to his face. "I was just seeing if any of my friends were still around."

Feeling the need to be rescued. Well, she should. Little girls should not go around picking up homeless men.

"Maybe they're still perusing the auction table." He cut a bite of roast and shoved it between his lips. "This is delicious."

"Good." She seemed preoccupied. "Would you excuse me for a moment?" She scooted back her chair and left the table.

Or, she could simply run away.

He watched her hurry over to the auction area and wondered if she would even come back.

He was scraping the last of the gravy off his plate with a roll when she returned.

"How's the bidding going?" he asked.

"I'm not sure." She sat back down.

He dabbed his mouth with the napkin. "Are you in charge of it?"

"No. But, I've donated several high-end items that aren't doing as well as I'd hoped." She shrugged and sipped her water. "So, how was it?" She asked, nodding to his empty plate.

"Great." He slapped his stomach in satisfaction. "But it's late and I really must be going."

"Oh. Okay." Disappointment filled her eyes.

"But," he leaned toward her in a conspiratorial manner. "Before I go, *I* have a couple of questions."

"Shoot."

"What's the gag, lady? Why am I really here?"

Jill blinked and stared, her deep tawny gaze locking with his. She licked her lips and swallowed.

"No gag."

"Then what are you doing flirting with a homeless man off the streets of New York City? Where is your father, for God's sake? Or, a brother? You need someone to watch out for you."

He tossed his napkin on the table and stood.

An angry gleam filled her eyes as she shot from her seat. "I don't know what you have to be so huffy about. Is it so wrong to offer a man a little warmth and a hot meal? Look around you. I'm surrounded by throngs of people. What could you possibly do to me?"

"Plenty, lady."

Living on the streets had been an eye-opening experience. He'd seen his share of young women, teenagers peddling themselves for money, going places they shouldn't. Dangerous places.

"Trust me, if you'd tried anything," she raised an expressive brow. "I'd have you flat-backed on the floor in seconds."

He stared at her trying to picture such a scenario. Smothering a grin, he eyed her, hoping to give as good as he got. "Don't you understand that someone like you shouldn't befriend a street person, a strange man twice your size? I suppose you pick up hitch-hikers, too?"

"I may be small in stature, but that doesn't mean I'm helpless. I also realize I look a lot younger than my twenty-five years, but I can't help that. And I'll have you know, my father is perfectly fine with who I am and how I'm living my life. But..." She pursed her lips and ran her finger along the edge of the tablecloth.

Suddenly, she was the most adorable thing he'd ever seen.

"Yes. Continue."

She raised her gaze to his. "He'd be furious if he knew what I'd done tonight." She tugged on her scarf, twisting and turning it around her fingers. "I come from a very loving and wonderful family. And, I do have a brother."

"Who'd also be furious?"

"He's younger than me."

Honest and forthright. Little Miss Jillian Jeffrey fashion designer was not like any other woman he'd ever known. Way too gullible, but he had to admit that did add to her charm. She'd captivated him from the moment she'd offered him the overcoat.

He gazed at this enchanting, brown-eyed girl and had the strongest desire to get to know her. In another life, he'd most definitely figure out a way for the two of them to spend the rest of the evening together. But, under his present circumstances, that was impossible.

"Thank you for dinner." He pushed his chair under the table and lifted his backpack.

"Wait. Let me at least give you something for another meal."

In her haste, she practically dumped the contents of her sequined purse onto the table. As she reached into her clutch, out slid a tube of lipstick, and a check for – good Lord. He blinked and stared... Twenty thousand dollars.

"That's not necessary," he said.

Ignoring him, she pinched up a wad of bills and handed them to him.

"Stop. Please."

"But—"

He placed his hand firmly on her outstretched arm. "This meal and the warmth was more than enough. Thank you."

For a moment she held his gaze, then nodded and slipped the bills back into her purse.

"Oh." Her eyes widened as if she'd just remembered something. "Before you go, I need to introduce you to some of my friends."

Needs to?

She waved to a couple just leaving a nearby table. "Paul. Elaine."

But Paul and Elaine were already walking in the opposite direction. They either didn't hear her or chose to ignore her. A frown creased Jillian's forehead.

What a perplexing and engaging young woman.

"As delightful as this evening and you are, I really must be going," he said. "It's late and I don't want to lose my spot under the bridge."

"You live under a bridge?" She squeaked the words.

"Brooklyn Bridge. It's quite nice as far as bridges go. But, this week, I'll be moving to a tent city in an abandoned subway. It's a lot warmer and actually not that far from here. Only a couple of subway stops."

"Let me get you a room."

"Here?" He couldn't resist asking.

Her eyes grew to the size of mushrooms.

"Just kidding." He lifted the coat off the chair next to him and handed it to her. "Thanks, but it's way too expensive."

"Oh, no." She shook her head. "Mark said you could have it."

"Mark?"

"Yes. My ex-boyfriend." She waved her small manicured hands through the air. "He has tons of money. Don't give it a second thought. The coat is yours."

"Well, in that case." He slipped his arms through the soft fabric and slid it over his shoulders. He gently clasped her warm fingers, then raised her hand to his lips. "Beggars really can't be choosers, can they?"

A twinge of sorrow flickered over her upturned face. And he wondered how this lovely innocent had survived in such a city. Immensely touched by her sincerity, he held her hand *and* her gaze longer than he should have. "Goodnight, Princess."

"Hey, Jill."

Jill's head snapped around at a lady's approach.

"What a great turnout tonight. I see your striped leggings finally brought in a pretty penny. That Pennington woman and Julia Simms were in a battle for them."

The tall blonde smiled at him.

"Hi, I'm Sandra," she gushed.

"Phil," he said. "A pleasure." He glanced at Jill who certainly looked like a teen entering puberty next to the full-figured woman standing in their midst.

"I'm sorry, Sandra. I'd ask you to join us, but as you can see Phil is just about to leave."

"That's okay. Donald is getting the car from valet parking, so, I need to scoot. Good job on that bet by the way."

Jill cast a nervous glance in his direction.

"What bet?" he asked.

"Our Jill scored huge tonight." A small laugh trickled from Sandra's red lips. "Her ex bet she couldn't get some hobo off the street to spend an hour with her." She winked at Jill who'd turned quite pale.

His heart all but stopped. "Hobo. Now there's a word I haven't heard in ages." He forced a smile and locked eyes with Jill who'd now gone deathly white. "That's our Jill, all right." He played along even though he was angry as hell. "How much was it for, again?"

"Twenty thousand delicious dollars."

He thought of the check inside Jill's purse.

Sandra slapped her hands together, then ran her gaze over his clothing. She fingered the lapels of his coat. "Nice," she purred. "Except for the shoes." Sandra scrunched up her nose and shook her head just as her iPhone dinged.

Saved by the cell.

"It's Donald. See you Jill. Nice meeting you, Phil."

Speechless, Jill stared at him, her small hands clutched tightly against her stomach.

"Twenty thousand an hour, huh? Since I was here two, I'd say you got cheated."

"Please. It's not what you think."

"I'm sure it isn't." He hoisted his backpack onto his shoulder.

Tears filled her eyes. "It's for charity—"

"Now that's touching, but seriously, there's no need to cry. I'm a big boy." He tapped the end of her nose. "Thanks for dinner." He grinned, feeling anything but happy, and strode from the room.

Cameron's eyes smarted from the cold blast as he entered the street. He didn't take kindly to being duped—especially by a supposedly, wide-eyed, innocent.

He hoofed it to Lexington and Fifty-Third and took the subway to High Street and The Brooklyn Bridge.

Twenty thousand. So people like Jillian Jeffrey could line their already fur-lined coats, with even more of what they don't need. Sure it's for charity. He scoffed a laugh. The Jillian Jeffrey Charity. He thought of the good that money could do for the homeless. But the check had been made out to *her.* He clenched his teeth against the raw anger that flared in his gut.

Wealthy. Spoiled. Brat.

Then it hit him… Jeffrey.

He thought he'd heard the name before. And he'd place his own bet she was one of the Jeffreys of Scarsdale. He'd heard about them. Old Money. Recently moved back to New York. He shook his head. Now it all made sense. He huffed out a frustrated breath. More socialites. Just what the city needed.

The bridge was quiet as he made his way to his spot. Eddie was already snoring when Cam arrived.

"Phil? That you?"

"Yeah, buddy. Sorry to disturb you."

"It's okay." Eddie ducked back into his cardboard tent.

Cam tossed his backpack inside his makeshift home and crawled through the small opening. He'd positioned the lean-to to keep most of the wind out, allowing the warmth of the small fire near the opening to take off most of the winter chill. He hunkered against the concrete wall, then pulled his laptop from the backpack, plugged his Verizon Air Card into the USB port and logged on.

Thankful to be done with them, he tossed the cheap, drug-store eyeglasses aside. After he pulled up his current Eagle Eye article, he typed in the evening's information while it was fresh on his mind. He'd spent most of the month gathering info and hadn't written the first word. The article was due in less than a week and he'd put off writing it long enough. Frankly, he'd been stuck and unsure of the direction the article should go. Until this evening, when the answer came out of nowhere in the form of one Miss Jeffrey of Scarsdale.

Two hours with her had provided the theme he'd been searching for. Just when he'd begun to think not all socialites were out for themselves, this young woman had proven once again that they actually *were.* The two hours in her company had been two of the best he'd experienced in a long while. At first, he'd found her charming and adorable. But sadly, she'd turned out to be like all the rest. And thanks to him, twenty thousand dollars richer.

Cam's fingers flew across the keyboard.

Take the up and coming teen girl fashion designer, Jillian Jeffrey of JJ Designs…

Focused. Direct. Slicing and dicing his target with precision. For a moment he hesitated, fingers hovering over the keyboard. His next words could be interpreted as especially cruel. Naming her could ruin her career. Should he stop? Temper his next words?

No.

But he would lessen the blow by adding examples of other such abuses by the so-called, well-meaning in the city.

One hour later, laptop stowed away, he settled back into the down sleeping bag, his only luxury during his undercover work. He tucked his arm underneath his head and blew out a breath.

His targets got everything they deserved. Usually at this point in an article, he felt good about what he'd written, but for some reason, exposing the doe-eyed beauty didn't sit well with him. In her case, he wasn't sure if it was his emotions thinking or his brain. Tonight he'd let it sit and see if he felt differently about naming her in the morning.

Burdened by the things he'd witnessed over the past three weeks, it was good to finally get them down in a thought-provoking manner. Until he'd lived it himself, he'd had no idea there were so many teenagers on the streets. The teen girls were especially heartbreaking to see. The problem was certainly more than he could handle in a major expose′. Wiser minds would have to solve this one.

His job was to simply make it known.

CHAPTER THREE

"Jill, what colors do you want the spring vests?" Jill's assistant, Amy Stallings, popped her head through the side opening to her office area. "Production is still waiting."

"Oh, Amy, I'm sorry." She rummaged through the swatches on her worktable. "It's such a mess when I'm designing."

"It's a mess when you're not."

Jill stopped foraging through the many stacks and gave her assistant the evil eye.

Amy grinned.

Jill pushed another stack of fabric samples aside. "I don't know where my brain is today." Actually, she did. It was on a tall, scruffy bearded street person that she'd hurt. A sharp pang dinged her heart. She could still see the look of disgust on his face. The blatant mockery in his icy-blue stare. No one had ever looked at her with such contempt. Worse. She'd actually deserved it.

It was strange, but until the end, she'd so enjoyed the two hours she'd spent in his company. Underneath those ill-fitting clothes and disheveled appearance, was an intelligent, articulate, and thoughtful man. Hard to believe someone with those qualities could ever become homeless. Frankly, the more she thought about it, the more she questioned his story. Would a homeless person smell all leather and lemony? Except for the hint of campfire smoke, it was quite appealing. And those eye lashes—

"Jill? What is up with you? You've been mooning around all week."

Jill blinked and snatched up the color samples. "I'm not mooning around." Irritated at herself, she handed the swatches to Amy. "Here you go. The top five are for the vests."

"Perfect. How are the skirt leggings coming? Best idea you've had, by the way."

"Thanks. I'm close, I promise. And again, I'm sorry. I honestly don't know where I'd be without you."

"I know. I'm so perfect. Hold on while I straighten my halo." Amy raised her hands over her head, and adjusted the invisible corona.

Jill laughed. "Go ahead, make fun of your boss. But, you know I'm such a mess when it comes to the business side of things."

"And I'm the last person one would call artistic. So we're perfect for each other." She raised her eyes heavenward and disappeared from the doorway.

After Amy left, Jill slouched back in her chair. No doubt about it, Mark had seduced her with such a huge sum of money. But she couldn't blame him for her own impulsive action to use the man. She could've refused. But how do you say no to twenty thousand dollars?

She'd obsessed over those last heart sickening moments and Sandra's ill-timed remarks all week. Had thought seriously about going back this weekend to see if he might be on the same corner. It saddened her to think of him living under the Brooklyn Bridge. It was Steve all over again.

* * *

Cameron was never certain if the aluminum lawn chair would hold together, considering the broken straps in the seat and back. He lowered his weight expecting this would be the moment it would finally give way and send him to the ground. He'd picked it up curbside next to someone's trash bin. Scavenging had almost become second nature to him.

Almost.

Admittedly, half of it had come from his dad's basement, but the ratty chair, beat-up Coleman stove, and the mix and match camping supplies were curbside finds. All of which he'd planned to will to Eddie when his undercover gig was over, along with a tent and enough propane to get him through the winter.

He'd just gotten comfortable in front of the open fire when he noticed a young girl. He hadn't seen her since his first week in the tent city and wondered if she'd taken his advice and gone home. She was fifteen and had run away supposedly from an abusive stepfather.

Cam had searched for her the day after he'd met her to see if she'd consider going to the police for protection. He knew someone in child services who'd be willing to help her find a safe environment until she turned eighteen. He'd actually set up the meeting, had the details worked out, then the girl had disappeared. Until now. She still had that scared rabbit look about her, like the first time he'd seen her.

He watched her attempt to set up an army-green pup tent a few yards from his lean-to. He had every intention of speaking to her again, but decided to wait until she got set up. He didn't want her running off. When she began to struggle with one of the stakes, she paused and glanced around the area.

He caught her eye, stood, and crossed the dormant patch of dirt. "Here. Let me help with that." He took the hammer and the stake from her fingers before she could object. "The ground is pretty much frozen this time of year." He hunched down beside her and deftly hammered in the last two stakes. "There. That should hold nicely."

"Thanks." Her voice was soft and low. Almost a whisper.

He stood while watching her, hoping she'd at least look at him. Eventually, his persistence to stand and say nothing paid off. After a full thirty seconds of hugging her torso, she shyly glanced up at him.

"Hey, I remember you," she said.

"And I remember you." He stuck out his gloved hand. "The name's Phil."

"Hi." Her grasp was barely one at all.

Without gloves, her hands must be near frozen. He slipped his off and handed them to her.

"No thanks. I have some in my backpack."

"Well, I'd put them on if I were you. And sleep in them. It gets awfully cold here at night."

She nodded. He noticed she'd not given him her name. Runaway 101. Never tell anyone your name, at least, not your real one.

"I haven't seen you around lately. I thought you might have gone back home."

She shook her head. "I was at a shelter for a while. But this man, he...*creeped* me out." She lifted a shoulder in a half-hearted shrug. "So I left."

"Sounds like leaving was the right thing to do." When she didn't respond, he continued. "So. You got a name?" he asked, anyway.

She glanced down and to her right. "L... Lisa."

"Nice to meet you, Lisa"

She kept her eyes lowered.

"You hungry? Do you have any food?"

"A little." She raised her gaze back to his. "I grabbed two slices at Toni's Pasta Bar. A couple had just left. The pizza was still warm."

"Sounds like perfect timing." He smiled.

"Not really. I'd been watching them. That's how I've been getting food."

"Yeah. It beats digging through trash cans."

His gut churned. He'd never get used to this. Kids scrounging for food on the street—in the cold.

"There's a fire over there if you want to warm up." He kept up the conversation, hoping to find out more about her.

"No thanks." Without a backward glance, she ducked underneath the tent flap, then zipped it shut.

He ambled back to his own tent and sat down. He stared into the fire and thought of the hundreds of other runaways in the city like Lisa and the overwhelming impossibility of helping them all. Anger and frustration gnawed deep in his gut. Well, he'd be damned if this one slipped through the cracks. He pulled out his cell phone, then shot off an email to his contact in child protective services.

CHAPTER FOUR

Jill applied pink gloss to her lips, then glanced at her watch. Her kid brother, Jamey, would be arriving soon. She'd promised him a weekend in New York to celebrate his upcoming sixteenth birthday. Post-Thanksgiving was the perfect time to be in the city when Christmas decorations glowed from every corner.

She looped the thin leather strap of her Brighton purse over her head, then headed downstairs to wait for Jamey in the lobby. Just as she stepped off the elevator, her brother pushed through the double glass doors.

"Jamey!"

He grinned and enveloped her with a big hug.

"I swear you keep getting taller every time I see you," she said.

Over the years his hair had gotten darker and his adoring eyes from childhood had grown sincere and honest, but still held their familiar twinkle when the two of them shared a joke. Jamey's height and good looks made him appear much older than his sixteen years.

"You ready for a night on the town?"

"Absolutely."

She looped her arm through his and together they pushed through the doors that led to the street.

After standing in line for twenty minutes at the Shake Shack, Jill and Jamey ordered burgers and fries. Jamey reached inside his jacket and pulled out his money clip.

"Not on your life, little brother. I told you, since I can't go home next Sunday for your birthday, this weekend is my treat."

He shoved his money back into his pocket. "You get no argument from me."

After dinner, they took a cab to central park and The Plaza. Once Jill paid the taxi, they got out near the giant bush in the center of the square. Glistening with thousands of twinkle lights, it was one of her favorite spots in the city.

As they headed down the street, Jill couldn't help but glance to the street corner where she'd first met Phil. It was empty. Well, not exactly empty. Throngs of people were strolling by that very spot, except for the one person she'd hoped would be standing there.

"Looking for someone?" Jamey said.

She nodded. "Sort of."

He eyed her doubtfully. "You either are or you're not."

"I met someone there over a week ago and I was hoping he might be there tonight."

She told him most of the story, and about the bet, but that was all.

"There was something about him," she said. "I don't think he really could have been a homeless person. I mean, he was sharp and a perfect gentleman at dinner. The guy knew what fork to use."

"You had dinner with a homeless man? Wait until Mom and Dad hear about this."

"Under no circumstances are you to breathe a word of this to them."

"I may be sixteen, but even I know this is crazy."

She bit her lower lip. "Wanna help me find him?"

"Thought you'd never ask." He grinned and glanced around the area. "Where do we begin?"

"The last time I was with him, he said something about moving to an abandoned subway nearby. I've been doing some research and there's one exactly two subway stops from here."

"Let's go."

* * *

Cameron stood in front of Toy Lin's Tattoos while holding his "Will Work for Food" sign. The location sat conveniently across the street from the subway entrance to his temporary digs.

His goal today—compare this side of town to the high rollers on the east side. During his time undercover, most people ignored his existence and avoided all eye contact. He and others like him were invisible even in this part of town. Jobs in this area only paid minimum wage, so he wasn't the least bit surprised he hadn't gotten the first dollar or offer of food.

Truthfully, he hoped to God no one would actually take him up on that, as he had a ham and cheese hoagie waiting in his backpack and a looming deadline that needed his attention.

As he shuffled from one foot to the other he thought about the last man that had given him work. After he'd swept three floors of the man's warehouse, said man fed him a peanut butter and jelly sandwich and a bag of stale chips for his efforts. When he'd eyed the guy with his 'are you kidding me' expression, the jerk threatened to call the police if Cam didn't leave.

Cam shivered and zipped his jacket as high as it would go. He'd give it another few minutes, then hit the computer. As he stood there pondering whether or not he would reveal the man's warehouse address in his article, he spied a familiar figure emerging from the entrance to the tent city subway across the street.

Well, if it wasn't little miss socialite herself. She was arm in arm with a tall young man who looked about sixteen or seventeen. He shook his head. So, she'd brought reinforcements. Did she actually think *the boy* could protect her? The men underground probably took one look at that baby face of his and—

Wait. Were they arguing?

The young man stopped and grabbed Jill's upper arm, halting her mid-stride. She turned toward him and threw out her free arm like she was trying to explain something. She kept looking back over her shoulder at the entrance to the subway, then back at the young man. The kid shook his head and yanked her away from the subway steps, marching her none to gently back down the block. She had to practically run to keep up with his long strides.

Good for you, kid.

* * *

"Jamey Jeffrey. Let me go this instant." Jill panted as she hustled alongside of her brother. "I mean it. I have to catch my breath."

Jamey stopped, but didn't let go of her arm. "Gosh, Jill. The man's not one of your stray kittens. Dad would kill me if I'd let you stay down there."

"Since when do you *let me* do anything? I'm twenty-five years old."

"And five-foot-two."

She shook her head. "Now you're sounding like *him*.

"Who?"

"Phil. My homeless man."

"Your homeless... Would you listen to yourself?"

She yanked her arm from Jamey's hold and proceeded to walk down the street. "Homeless people aren't criminals, you know. And for your information, I can take care of myself."

"Well, I can't. Did you see how that one guy came at me? I thought my basketball days were over."

"He didn't come after you. And since when did you become so melodramatic?"

"Oh, forget it." He shook his head.

"Wait. Look." She pointed her finger at his face.

"What?"

"Right there." She grinned. "You looked just like Dad then."

Jamey rolled his eyes and playfully slapped her hand away.

"I guess one of us had to turn out responsible and sensible." Jill grabbed both his hands and gazed fondly up at him. "Too bad Mom and Dad will never know."

"If that's your way of securing my silence on the matter, my lips are sealed. But only if you promise you'll stop looking for this guy."

"Fine."

They caught a taxi back to Fifth Avenue and Central Park. As they strolled to the next corner, Jill glanced around at the variety of street venders. "How about a pizza slice or a hot pretzel. You can't come to New York City and not get a hot pretzel."

Minutes later, Jamey slathered mustard on the warm, salty dough. As he bit into it, he closed his eyes as if savoring the taste. Jill motioned him over to a nearby park bench.

Central Park and the Plaza were hangouts for tourist and native alike. Since moving here, the Plaza was one of her favorite spots in the city. There were much more elaborate and expensive hotels for sure, but she loved the history and romance of the place. And you couldn't beat the location.

For a few moments they ate in silence and people-watched. But truthfully, she was on the lookout for one particular person.

From this seat she had the perfect view of *his* corner. Jamey had no idea of course and she had no intention of telling him.

She wondered when her brother had become so sensible. Growing up in Paige Point, she'd never thought of him that way. Maybe it was simply the fact that New York was such a massive city, and so completely different from their tiny fishing village. It was probably a good thing he was being careful. The world could be a dangerous place and New York certainly had specific pockets to avoid.

The weekend ended all too soon, and Sunday afternoon, Jill accompanied him to the LaGuardia airport for his flight home.

"Promise you'll stop looking for that Phil guy?"

She scrunched up her nose. "Okay. Fine." But Jill knew even as she said the words it would be a promise she'd have a hard time keeping.

CHAPTER FIVE

Monday morning, cradling a mug of hot coffee in her hand, Jill stood in front of her closet eyeing the menagerie of color and styles staring back at her. An assortment of pinks, blues, and oranges combined in a variety of stripes, checks, and plaids and suddenly she felt like she had absolutely nothing to wear.

She pushed the clothes from one side to the other. Was there nothing in here for a professional businesswoman?

She sighed and yanked off the next thing that touched her fingers, promising herself a shopping spree at Bloomingdale's sometime that week.

She slipped on the orange and pink corduroy outfit and gazed at her reflection in the bedroom mirror. Could she help it if she lived in the mind of teenage girls? Sure, when she hit forty it would probably become a problem. But right now she was twenty-five and teenage girls were her bread and butter.

At the office, she was met with a flurry of activity and decisions that needed her attention. *This* is what she lived for. Reveled in.

As the day went along her mind drifted to her street guy. Even hidden behind that offbeat, bohemian appearance, he was gorgeous. Too bad about the wire-rim eyeglasses, though. Contact lenses would be useless living on the streets, unless he had access to daily running water. Even then, it could be difficult to manage.

She thought of his wavy hair and how it touched his shirt collar, just so. She fingered her own collar as her thoughts continued to roam. A little too much facial hair for her tastes, but still... She sighed, and shook her head at her wayward thoughts. What was the matter with her? She shot from her chair and inspected the reams of fabric Amy had left on the design table and got to work.

But as the day wore on, she found herself fantasizing about what he must look like underneath all that hair. She bet heavenly. She twirled a number two pencil between her fingers. Clean-shaven or a bit of stubble might be nice. She imagined he housed a well-fit form underneath those ill-fitting clothes of his. A Hugo suit and Hermes tie would look especially nice on him. And hair cut short and neat.

Phil commanded her thoughts much more than he should. But it was his eyes and the timbre of his voice that haunted her. This man was savvy, insightful. He had to be more than he'd let on. Or was it simply that she'd hoped so. She'd had high hopes for Steve as well and the thought that Phil could end up the same way saddened her. If only there was something she could do.

Amy popped in the doorway. "Just thought you'd want to know how much we raised at the fundraiser. Two thousand, forty-seven dollars."

"Not bad," Jill said. "And with Mark's donation we'll have twenty thousand more."

"What do you mean?" Amy's eyes flew wide open. "That's fantastic. How in the world did you swing that?"

"I appealed to Mark's sweeter side, of course." Jill batted her eyes.

"Ha, if that guy has a sweet side, it's news to me."

"I'll admit one does have to squint in order to see it."

"When's your meeting with Annie?"

"She's invited me to a luncheon tomorrow to meet the board members."

"With this donation, you're sure to get the position."

"I hope so."

Amy crossed her fingers and raised them in the air. "For good luck."

* * *

Anna Delany was even more beautiful than her photos. Jill tilted her head back and smiled at the tall, dark-haired founder of Like No Other. She'd worked with the international super model several times the past year and each time Annie seemed to grow more and more stunning.

"How do you do it?" Jill said.

"Do what?"

"Keep that glowing complexion of yours."

"Well, I could say it's from using some of the best health and beauty products in the world, but actually it's from years of protecting my skin from the sun's harmful rays. If the girls only take one thing from my sessions, I'd like it to be that one fact."

After a light lunch of shrimp salad, Annie stood and smiled down at Jill.

"Jill, it's wonderful to see you again. I understand you have some fabulous news for the board."

"I do." She stood and scanned the small group of professionals seated around the table. "My friends and I raised twenty-two thousand forty-seven dollars for LNO." She handed Annie the check as light applause fanned across the room.

After the meeting, Annie pulled Jill aside. "Jill I'd like for you to consider being on the board of LNO. At this time you're one of three we're looking at."

Jill's heart thudded. This was what she'd wanted. It was actually happening. "I don't quite know what to say, except thank you for thinking of me. But, I'm not sure, I mean—"

Annie fluttered her right hand through the air. "No rush. You don't have to decide right now. Just think about it." Annie offered a cheery smile and glanced at the departing board members. "As you can see, most of my board consists of older business men and women. All wonderful and fully capable, but I'd like someone younger who understands teenage girls. I think you'd be a terrific asset to the foundation. As you know, raising money has been a bit of a challenge over the past year because of this thing with Alex Langdon. Fundraising is critical to the success of an organization like ours, and what you've done in such a short amount of time is incredible."

"Well, I did have some help." *And I sort of blackmailed someone in the process, then shamelessly used a homeless man.* Jill forced a smile and nodded. "I promise, I'll think seriously about it. I'll have to weigh in my other responsibilities and design commitments. You understand."

"Of course. Sounds like your business is finally taking off."

"It seems so." Jill lifted her purse off the chair back and slung it over her shoulder. "Only verbal commitments at this point. I'll breathe a lot easier when something's on paper."

Twenty minutes later, Jill walked through her office building, then entered the elevator. She stared straight ahead at the elevator doors. What was wrong with her? Yesterday she'd have jumped at Annie's offer. Instead, guilt nagged her conscience, causing her to hesitate.

When the doors opened onto her floor, she didn't budge. Instead, she pressed the down button. This time she watched the lit floor numbers descend one digit at a time before the doors opened to the first floor.

She exited the building, crossed the street, then flagged the nearest cab to the Plaza. She quickly paid the fare and got out. Phil's corner near the park was empty. She glanced at her watch. Three-thirty. She ducked into Central Park Bistro and took a seat at the window. From here she'd have a good view of most of the corners in the area. Maybe he'd show up. She wanted the chance to explain about the bet. If she could clear the air with him she'd feel better about taking the position. She'd used him and, despite it being for a good cause, knew she'd done it for her own advancement.

She'd heard about the opening on LNO's board long after she'd been a volunteer. She'd so wanted that position and figured if she could raise enough money, then she'd at least have a chance at it. At first all she'd cared about was helping the foundation, and figured working with a world famous model and philanthropist would not only give her an elevated status in the city, but in the fashion district, as well.

Now she'd been invited to consider the position she most wanted, but in her heart knew she didn't deserve it. She gripped her coffee mug and gazed at the empty corner, reliving the scathing look in his eyes. Funny really, because at that very moment he'd assumed she was one of those 'the world at her feet, nose in the air' kind of women. He'd assumed the worst about her and it was her own stupid fault. And now it seemed she finally had what she'd wanted…after all, social standing *is* everything. Disgusted with herself, she stared out the window.

Oh, my gosh! That's him.

She quickly laid a five-dollar bill on the counter and left. She had to wait for the light to turn green before she could cross the wide street. Frustration mounted as she watched Phil's long strides take him farther and farther away from her.

Traffic flew by and Jill counted the seconds as she waited for the pedestrian walk light to appear on the screen. When the light changed, Jill ran across the four lanes, not once taking her eyes off Phil. He caught a cab and she immediately followed in another one. A few minutes later, she watched him enter the abandoned subway.

Jill paused at the top of the steps to catch her breath. Now that she was this close she hesitated. She'd day dreamed more than once of finding him underneath the Brooklyn Bridge. Explaining everything to him. But, now that she had the opportunity to speak to him, she wasn't so sure. She knew what he'd say, though. He'd say she was nuts. And she probably was.

It would be dark soon and even darker below, but if she didn't go now, she'd risk losing him. She squared her shoulders, doubled-looped her scarf around her neck, then proceeded down the steps to the underground.

CHAPTER SIX

A gut-churning stench rose in waves from the nasty concrete. Jill pulled her scarf over her nose and mouth as a mingling of cigarette smoke, cheap whisky and urine assailed her. Tents and cardboard lean-tos peppered the area. Men and women stood or sat huddled along the concrete wall. A few had lanterns, but most of the light came from the exposed bulbs overhead. Shocked at the inhuman conditions, she moved forward.

Her world consisted of glitz and glamour and the sight and smell looming for yards ahead both sickened and saddened her. As she stepped around a man eating from a tin can she noticed a middle-aged woman sitting against the wall, knees drawn to her chest taking a drag from a cigarette. No one seemed the least bit interested in Jill, which was a good thing. But no sooner had she thought that, a pair of dark eyes latched onto her and followed her like a haunted house portrait. Goosebumps trailed over her flesh. Heart thudding, she glanced away.

At that moment the light bulb over her head popped and blew out plunging that section of the platform into dark, eerie shadows. She halted mid-step, her sharp inhale drawing attention from those around her. She swallowed against the burning sensation inside of her throat and focused on the next light bulb just up ahead.

A ghostly figure lounging against the wall seemed to be eyeing her. Hard to tell as his face was in shadows, but she could tell she'd caught his attention. Her steps quickened keeping pace with her racing heartbeat. If only she hadn't acted so impulsively. At least she could defend herself if she had to, but it was foolish to put that fact to the test—here of all places. The man in shadow pushed his body from the wall and moved toward her.

That's it. She spun around and headed back toward the entrance. The urge to flee fueled her feet and she began to walk faster. The man followed. Fear clawed her chest. She held her breath.

Don't look back. Keep going.

All thoughts of finding Phil left and she picked up her pace. Heavy footsteps loomed behind her, matching her steps in speed and quickness. She had to get back to the street. When she spotted the stairs at the entrance, she walked even faster. The faster she walked, the faster he walked. Clutching her purse, she sprinted forward. Throat burning with each gulp of cold air, her heart drummed, drowning out everything except her need to escape.

A strong hand gripped her right arm.

A pathetic yelp escaped her lips. She elbowed the man's ribs and broke free.

"Jillian!"

Through the ear-buzzing noise, someone yelled her name, gripped her shoulders and spun her toward him. Legs shaking, she physically sagged. And if he released her she'd have slumped to the ground.

"What the heck are you doing here?" Discomfort creased his brow as he pressed his hand against his side.

They were standing in the area where the light had blown.

"Phil! Thank God." She stared into the intense face of her street bum, his longish hair and scruffy beard a welcome sight.

But, all the hair in the world could not conceal his complete surprise. If anything, it enhanced it. He pulled her to the next light bulb with such force that her feet lifted off the concrete.

Even though her body still trembled, relief strengthened her limbs. Otherwise, she'd have been mush. Phil smelled of leather, spice and smoke. Just like that night in the hotel ballroom. She inhaled deeply, savoring the moment, knowing this could have turned out a lot worse.

He kept his hand pressed to his rib cage. "Nice move, by the way."

"Thank you."

Phil put her away from him and looked down at her. "Are you absolutely out of your mind? You shouldn't be here." He shot a glance beyond her. "Much less, alone."

His eyes were ablaze with annoyance. He was wearing a down jacket and jeans.

"Where's your cashmere coat?"

He blinked. The sudden change in his expression was not lost on her. He actually looked befuddled.

"I…um, traded it. For this one."

"Oh. I suppose down is warmer than cashmere."

"Don't change the subject." He'd gotten complete control of the situation and glared at her.

"I guess it does seem crazy." She gazed at him and smiled. "Thank you for worrying about me."

He heaved a sigh and dropped his arms to his sides.

"Someone sure needs to." He shook his head and led her to a rusty, metal drum. He held his hands over the open fire. "What are you doing here?"

She raised her gloved hands to the flame. "I was across the street and I happened to see you. I caught a cab and followed you here."

"Why don't I believe you?"

"Okay." She cleared her throat. "I admit it. I've been looking for you. I was having coffee in the bistro near the park when I spotted you. So, I followed you here."

An incredulous expression crossed his face. "You do see the weirdness in this don't you?"

"I felt badly for what Sandra said last week."

"It was the truth, wasn't it?"

"To a point, but—"

"Look. An abandoned subway is no place for a spoiled socialite. This place is dangerous."

"You think I'm spoiled?"

"Yes and twenty thousand dollars wealthier."

"The twenty thousand was for charity."

"I guess that made what you did to me okay?"

"No. Of course not." She sighed. "Look, I admit that I've done fairly well for myself. But it hasn't always been that way."

"You're a Jeffrey. It's always been that way, sweetheart."

She pulled her hands away from the flame and clasped them to her chest. "What do you mean?"

"Wealthy, wrapped up in yourself, and according to the society pages, *One of New York City's wealthiest families back in town*," he mocked. "Everyone who's anyone in this city knows about the Jeffrey girls of Scarsdale."

"Girls?"

"Your sisters."

"Oh, of course, them." First Mark and now him. No wonder he had ill feelings toward her. He thought she was one of *those* Jeffreys.

"So, you think because of that you know me?"

"Not you personally, but…" He shrugged.

"When you've met one high society dame, you've met them all. Is that it?"

"Dame? Now there's a word." The corners of his mouth lifted. "First hobo and now dame. You and your friends should get out more."

For one second, all she saw was his to-die-for half-smile. That along with his disheveled appearance was quite a package.

"Well, according to your earlier comment, my *friends* and I get out plenty."

He gazed down at her. His crooked smile still played around his lips and his eyes held a sudden twinkle that disarmed her. But she couldn't help notice the note of disdain behind that charming twinkle. She'd used him, coaxed him into a glamorous environment, then humiliated him. It probably wouldn't make any difference as to what he thought of her, so let him think what he wanted.

* * *

"Does it really matter who you think I am? Isn't it enough that I made a mistake and that I want to make things right?"

"Look, I've known girls like you. Wealthy. Spoiled." *Brainless.* "Who think they can do anything and go anywhere without consequence."

"What's so wrong with wanting to help you?" Jill asked.

Phil shook his head. "Look around you, Princess. You come from money."

"Wealth is such a relative term."

"Tell that to those who don't have any. Look. *You* may have done well, but the rest of us are still under water."

"If you were under water you'd drown. But, I see steps over there. Take one step at a time and you're out."

"Just like that, huh? You're naïve if you think it's that simple."

"The way I see it is, if one person helps another, then that's one less underground. Look. I know we got off to a bad start."

"A bad start? You and I…we have no relationship. Nothing has started here."

But he may as well have saved his breath. She didn't miss a beat.

"I know I've insulted you," she continued. "I know in your position it doesn't matter why, but you can trust me when I say it was for a worthy cause. And I really want to help you."

He took her gloved hands in his. "It's quite noble. And I do appreciate it, but I don't need, nor do I want your help."

"How can you stand there and say that? You're living in a subway tunnel." She shot a glance over his shoulder. "And it's scary down here."

He didn't say a word. Just gave a look he hoped she'd understand. A look that told her he wouldn't budge. He knew she'd finally gotten the message when her sincere expression turned to one of disappointment.

She pulled her hands from his. "Fine. I get it. You don't want help from *any* Jeffrey." She practically spat the word and opened her purse. "At least let me give you a little something to get you back on your feet."

"Good Lord." Cam spoke with disgust, then took her by the arm and marched her up the stairs onto the well-lit, busy street. "What's your address?" He practically barked the question.

"It's 354 East Fifty-Seventh Street."

"Of course it is."

"It's not what you think."

"As you keep saying."

He flagged a taxi. If he didn't get her out of here, he might do something he'd later regret.

He held the door and waited until Jill settled into the back seat.

"Look. I can't deny that your heart's in the right place. But it's time for little do-gooders to be off the street." He ducked down and spoke to the driver. "Three-Fifty-Four East Fifty-Seventh Street."

He shut the door and stepped back.

"Driver, wait." Jill rolled down the window, never taking her eyes off Phil's face. Before he could straighten up, Jill pushed her upper body through the window, grabbed the front of his jacket, and tugged his face to hers. "You can do better than this, Phil," she whispered. "I just know it."

Should he tell her the truth? He tore his eyes from her probing ones, focusing on her parted lips instead. His mouth hovered mere inches above hers.

For a second all he could do was stare at her beautiful, up-turned face.

God help him. In one motion, he shoved her back through the window, until her backside was safely in the seat where she belonged.

He hit the car hood to send it on its way, then watched them drive down Fifth Avenue. He sucked in a harsh breath and held himself rigid until the taillights could no longer be seen.

He ran his hand through his hair. He needed a drink. He glanced at the stairs that led to the underground, but somehow a shot from Eddie's bottle of Old Crow turned his stomach. A harsh reminder of hugging the toilet during his Frat house party days. Nope. He'd spent over three weeks on this job and wanted, no needed, a *real* drink.

He briskly walked the two blocks to Kelley's Bar and Grill. When he entered the semi-dark space, he was met with what he'd come to call the 'you don't belong here' stare from the clientele. He made a mental note to add that to his article. Ignoring them, he moved toward the bar, then sat down.

An attractive brunette approached him. "What would you like?"

"McCallum 18."

She gave a skeptical glance, and shrugged. "You got it."

A moment later she set the bourbon in front of him. He took a sip, savoring the liquid gold. He'd had his fill of cheap whisky and wine and as much as he loved undercover work, would be glad when this assignment was over.

Cam threw back his head and downed another shot. What was it with that kid? Yeah, some kid. She'd lit a fire in his belly. Churned his gut into a thousand little pieces, doing all manner of wonderful things to his insides. He'd wanted to kiss her. To taste her pink upturned mouth. But then he'd remembered the part he was playing in that moment. If she hadn't been the target of his latest article, Cam would have kissed her, but Phil could not.

Why hadn't he just hauled her upstairs as soon as he'd seen her? That's what he should have done. But truthfully, he was intrigued. By her audacity and Lord help him, her perfectly formed little mouth and a dazzling smile that lit up her eyes like Christmas morning.

He eyed the liquid in his glass. Tonight was the second time Miss Jeffrey had gotten the better of him. Two times too many as far as he was concerned.

He rubbed his hand around the back of his neck, and motioned to the bartender for another one.

A buzz came from deep within his pocket. He pulled out his cell and looked at the caller ID. Dick Powel, his editor.

"How's the story coming?" Dick said.

"It's finished."

"Then send it."

"Can't. Not yet. I'm still debating about one of the facts."

"The all-seeing Eagle second guessing?" Dick chuckled. "That doesn't sound like you."

"I have until tomorrow evening."

"That's what you said last time. Until you resign, you still work for a real newspaper. I swear the way you push my limit is going to put me in the emergency room."

"Don't worry. I always make it on time."

"Don't worry, he says. Remember, I need it by six tomorrow, not minutes before we go to press."

"You'll get it."

"You're the best journalist at the *Post*, but if you're late again, you'll be a copy-editor for some fledgling small town newspaper."

"I love you, too, Dick."

"Remember. Six. Tomorrow."

"Got it."

He pressed end and as he shoved his phone in his pocket, it buzzed again. It was Ethan Knight.

"Well, if it isn't my favorite fledgling small town newspaper man."

"What?"

"Sorry." Cam chuckled. "Bad joke."

"It seems the path of the straight and narrow is a lot harder than I thought it would be," Ethan said.

"Don't tell me you're missing the bright lights of Orlando."

"Not one little bit."

"What's happening with the merger?" Cam fingered the shot glass.

"It's a go on their end, but I don't feel good about it. They want too much control."

"You don't sound too happy about it. I thought that's what you wanted?"

"The merger, yes, loss of control, no. It's not what I want, but it's the only lifeline this little paper has at the moment. Apalacha Key News has been in the Knight family four generations. This deal has been especially tough on my grandmother."

"I'm sorry."

"Yeah, she's heartbroken and all she keeps talking about is the old days and how this wouldn't happen on Jim's watch."

"Jim?"

"My father."

"Look. She's of a different generation. It's hard on them. Mergers are quite common."

"Yeah, yeah. So, how is the homeless article coming?"

"Sweetly, if I say so myself."

"The all-knowing Eagle Eye." Ethan chuckled.

"The best idea we ever had."

"I take no credit for that one," Ethan said. "It was all yours."

"Well, let's hope it gets syndicated. Then we can both celebrate."

"And who are you going to nail this time?"

Cam's breath caught in his throat. "I'm not sure…that is… This one's a young woman. At this point I'm thinking about keeping her identity a secret."

"Hey, if you're having doubts, I'd listen to yourself. My new motto… *When in doubt, don't.* My advice? Tread carefully with that toxin, one day it may come back to bite you and you just might find yourself without an antidote."

"Any more encouraging words?"

"Just saying, bro. But, listen. Have you set up a meeting with Anna Delany of Like No Other?"

"Not yet, why?"

"I really need you to write that article for her foundation."

"Since when are you a bleeding heart?"

"Let's just say, I owe her *and* her husband."

"And Miss Marsh?" Cam lifted his finger for the check. "How's that going?"

"Prickly as ever."

"Well, good luck with that." Cam chuckled. "And I'll call your friend. I'm due for a fluff piece."

"Hey, none of that now. I think you'll be surprised to discover Like No Other foundation is anything but."

"Fine. It'll be a nice change after a month on the streets."

"Great. I'll let her know, and you two can work out the details when you meet."

"Okay. Talk soon."

Cam slapped a twenty on the bar, then left. He glanced at his watch. It was nine p.m. His stomach growled and he realized he hadn't eaten since noon, when a gray-haired elderly lady on Seventeenth gave him her tuna fish sandwich and chips with a, 'God bless you, son.'

He smiled at the memory. Most people her age ignored the homeless. But she'd walked up and handed him her sack lunch with a, 'Wish I could do more.'

He zipped his jacket and hustled down the street toward his cardboard home, the hint of bourbon heating his throat with every breath he took. He stopped by an all-night pizza kiosk, bought a large slice of pepperoni, folded it in half and continued walking.

His mind went to Jill and her honey doe eyes and found her intense, eager-to-help manner hard to justify with her earlier motive to use him for some party joke. Charity or not, using a homeless man was not cool.

He thought about the article and how much it would hurt her. With a few minor changes, no one would ever know it was Jill he was referring to, not even her. But it was too late for that. She'd still used a homeless man for gain and that type of action on the part of the well-to-do was the crux of his piece. He would sure hate to be her in the near future.

He paused at a trashcan, shoved the last bite of pepperoni into his mouth, then tossed the napkin, wondering not for the first time, if Jill Jeffrey were brave or just plain stupid.

CHAPTER SEVEN

Jill opened the door of the brownstone and stepped inside to the comforting warmth of the house. She unwound her scarf and slipped out of her coat, tossing both on the entry hall table.

She'd berated herself most of the taxi-ride home marveling at her own stupidity. She paused to gaze at her reflection in the foyer mirror. "What? Did you think you could drag him into the car with you? What were you thinking, grabbing him like that?" She threw her hands over her face and moaned. What did it matter? She'd never see him again.

She kicked off her shoes and padded to the kitchen. After making a cup of tea, she returned to the living room and curled up on the sofa. It was time to refocus, to get on with her life and career.

She glanced around the spacious apartment. A brownstone in this location had been financially out of her reach, but she'd lucked out when a friend of a friend needed someone to house sit for a couple of years while the owner worked in London. She couldn't have been happier, said yes and moved in. She'd been fortunate. Heaven had smiled on her for sure. But what about Phil? Why didn't heaven smile on him as well as all the rest of those she'd seen in the subway?

She blew softly across the hot liquid before bringing the cup rim to her lips. Phil's piercing blue eyes haunted her thoughts. Gorgeous, unforgettable, they looked straight into her soul. She wiggled down into the seat and hugged the warm mug to her chest. The aroma of sweet chamomile drifted upward, soothing her jumbled thoughts.

What was it about him that tugged at her so? Steve's death and months of volunteering at the soup kitchen played a part for sure. But this thing with Phil went deeper than that. She eased a hot sip of tea between her lips.

She knew it was foolish, even reckless to tag after a homeless man like some lost puppy. But was he homeless? Too many things told her otherwise. His white-tooth smile for one. And how could a homeless man know all about the Jeffreys of Scarsdale? Especially since they'd only recently moved back. Would a homeless man even read the society pages? Even her own research revealed very few photos of the family and the ones she could fine showed only partial images of the sisters. So how could Phil know so much about them?

She set her teacup on the side table, scooted comfortably down on the sofa, and closed her eyes, the aroma of leather and spice heavy on her mind.

* * *

The hum of the large newspaper could be heard from every hallway in the building. Cam loved the energy and vibe of the place, which at times, seemed more home to him than his own apartment.

Friday morning, he entered the third-floor offices dressed in jeans and a thick sweater and made his way across the floor to his cubical. With a cup of strong coffee at his elbow, he spent the next couple of hours cleaning up his article. After one last read-through, he attached it in an email to Dick, then hit send.

The article was on the craziest things people have seen on their way to work and he was happy to be done with it. Cameron Phillips was known for his fluff, but highly entertaining articles for several years now. The perfect cover for Eagle Eye's serious by-lines. What better way to keep his Eagle Eye identity a secret? No one would link the fluff articles of Cameron Phillips with the candid, no-holds-barred, columns by The Eagle.

He drummed his fingers along the top of the desk and took a moment to savor his last hours at the paper. Most of his colleagues hovered over their laptops feverishly typing under deadline. Some were on the phone following up on a lead. No doubt about it, a part of him would certainly miss this place.

Dick Powel approached. "You know, there's no rush in cleaning out your desk."

Cam rocked back in his ergonomic chair. "I was just thinking about you."

"Sure you were." Dick smiled. "Any chance you'd consider changing your mind? Freelance is not always the dream job people think."

"There are some other things I want to focus on right now. But, thanks for letting me keep my weekly article coming after I'm gone."

"Not at all. Our readers love it. With all the bad news in the world, it's nice to offer something crazy and lighthearted."

Cam nodded.

"What are your plans?"

"I'm thinking of going into partnership with a friend who owns a small town newspaper." Cam gathered up some stray papers and stood. "He just doesn't know it yet."

Dick raised a dark brow. "You, small town? Sorry, but I don't see it."

"Hey, did I say I was moving there?"

Dick gave a lopsided grin and held out his hand. "Well, good luck. I look forward to your next piece. And remember, there's always a place for you here."

Cam gripped Dick's hand. "Thanks. Let me know if I need to make any changes to my article before I go."

Dick shot a quick glance around the area and lowered his voice. "And the Eagle article?"

"Almost finished."

"Remember—"

"I know. Six tonight."

Dick nodded and walked off.

Cameron sat down and opened his article on New York's homeless. He still hadn't thought of an appropriate title. Brushing that aside, he dove in.

He scrolled down to the paragraph where he'd mentioned the fundraiser gala and Jill specifically. Dissecting each word, he carefully reread it. He sat back and scraped his hand across his mouth. Without compromising the heart of the piece, he could take out her name and that of her company. At the moment, that was the best he could do.

As an investigative reporter, you lay out all the facts. You name names. "And just who are you trying to convince?" He stared at the highlighted words on the screen while his right index finger hovered over the delete key.

Since when do you cave to a beguiling young woman? To an engaging twinkle in the biggest brown eyes you've ever seen?

Shaking his head, he blew out a breath. There's a first time for everything. He wouldn't use her name, but would leave the facts. If she read the article, she alone would know it was her he'd referred to. And if anyone else figured it out, then that would be her problem.

He hit delete and the words, *Jillian Jeffrey of JJ Designs,* disappeared.

* * *

Jill was seated at her worktable going over her sketches with Amy when Mark waltzed in.

"Well if it isn't Mr. Wonderful." Amy straightened up to her full height as if ready for battle. "Isn't this a bit early for you?"

"Hello, Amy. I see your tongue is still as sharp as ever." He winked and Amy pulled a face.

"From both your contented, almost happy expressions, I see you haven't seen the expose´."

"What expose´?" Jill and Amy spoke simultaneously.

"On the condition of the homeless in the city." He cocked a brow. "*The Invisible Man.*"

"And what does that have to do with me?" Jill said.

Mark had the paper opened to the article and handed it to Jill. "I think the infamous Eagle Eye has mentioned you."

"The who?"

"The all-seeing Eagle Eye," he said. "Don't tell me you haven't heard of him."

"I haven't heard of him." She took the paper from Mark and scanned the first few paragraphs. After a moment she looked pointedly at him. "I don't see anything."

"Keep reading."

Jill sighed and continued. Ten seconds later her mouth went dry. She glanced up at two faces, one expectant and the other sporting a knowing, albeit, slight smile.

"Well. What's it say?" Amy asked.

Jill swallowed, then read the next paragraph out loud.

"*…Take the up and coming and hottest new designer of teen-girl fashion. Small in stature she packs quite a punch especially when* *challenged to a bet. Witnesses say she and her friends at the latest charity gala used a homeless man to raise money for their holiday charity fling. Sadly, it is the practice of some to humiliate those they say they wish to help. And, for what? Sport?…"*

Jill's insides withered. "I can't read any more."

"That's terrible," Amy said.

Jill pressed her fingers to her temples. "Who is this…this bottom feeder?"

"Let me see that." Amy snatched the article from Jill's limp fingers.

"How could he even have known about the bet?" Jill glared at Mark. "Unless *you* told him?"

"I didn't tell him."

"But, I'm sure you're enjoying this," Jill said.

"Somewhat." He grinned. "My pockets are twenty thousand lighter because of you."

"Honestly, you and your millions. Go get a job!"

"I have a job."

"Working two days a week for Daddy does *not* count."

"I don't get it?" Amy placed the newspaper back on Jill's desk. "What's the big deal? It was for charity."

Jill shook her head, stared at the article and frowned. "He must have been there, covering the gala. And…and overheard someone talking about it. Sandra sure found out in a hurry." Jill cringed, and splayed her hands over the newspaper. "Sandra's big mouth. Everyone must have been talking about it. The only person who knew…" Jill slowly turned her gaze to Mark. "You!"

"Okay. Fine. I did tell Sandra."

"This was between you and me." Jill slapped her open palm on the desk. "Now she's blabbered it all over the place."

"You don't really think I'd risk twenty grand on your word alone to fulfill your side of the bet, do you?"

"Don't you have anything better to do with your life?" Jill jumped to her feet and began to pace. "I still don't see how he could have found out about Phil."

"Phil?"

"The homeless man he mentions in the article. As far as I know, Phil hadn't had a chance to meet anyone, except Sandra. He left right after she spilled the beans."

"Was anyone else around?" Amy asked. "Anyone sitting nearby?"

"Yeah, but I don't remember who. No one I knew personally."

"Well, maybe one of them is this Eagle Eye person," Amy said. "He overheard your conversation and jumped to his own conclusions."

"Wait. I did leave Phil alone for a couple of minutes. Someone could have talked to him then." Jill's shoulders slumped. "But, how could this man gather that much info in two minutes?"

"This guy writes in-your-face pieces," Amy said. "He's pretty new on the scene, but everyone reads his articles."

"Which means everyone will read this."

"The man's not afraid to point fingers, that's for sure." Mark had taken back the paper and continued to peruse the article. "Rather enjoys it if you ask me."

"What happened to journalists getting all the facts before they publish anything?" Jill jabbed her index finger at her chest. "I wasn't interviewed."

"He must have talked to your street guy." Amy said. "Purely chance, I'm sure."

"That doesn't make me feel one whit better."

"I'll just write another check and this time make it out to the charity," Mark said. "Then you can tear the other one up."

"It's too late." Jill glanced between Mark and Amy. "I've already deposited the money and presented a check to LNO at their board luncheon."

"Cheer up." Mark said. "Hopefully it will blow over in a day or so."

"I hope you're right." She clamped her teeth over her lower lip.

"Look, we think it might be you only because we *know* you," Amy said. "It sounds like you. But it doesn't mean it *is* you." Amy offered an encouraging smile. "I'm sure no one will even notice."

"Except people in our industry who, like you said, *know* me." Jill stopped and leaned her hip against the table. "I'm probably overreacting. Right? I mean, who reads newspapers anyway?" Except according to Amy, everyone read the Eagle Eye.

"Right. Well, I'll…uh…leave you two ladies to mourn." Mark strode from the office without a backward glance.

"Does he usually bring such happy news?"

"Mark's okay. I think I finally have him figured out." Jill pushed herself from the table and sat back down.

"Yeah, he's a big kid, completely irresponsible and the best looking thing this side of the Mississippi."

"Oh, my gosh!" Jill stared at her friend in amazement. "You like him."

"Now you're talking nonsense."

"It's okay, you know. I don't mind."

Amy plopped down on the chair across from the worktable. "I know. You're a good person, Jill. Don't worry about that stupid article. And forget what I said about everyone reading Eagle Eye. Just because I read it—"

"Amy. It's okay."

Amy picked up the newspaper and gnawed on her bottom lip. "Do you think this could affect the board position?"

Jill nodded. "It could certainly affect my chances. Annie will withdraw the offer if she gets wind of this. And I wouldn't blame her. She's had enough trouble."

At that moment the phone rang causing both women to jump.

Amy picked up the receiver. "Hello, JJ Design's. Amy Stallings speaking."

"Yes." Amy's eyes widened. "Jill Jeffrey will be happy to meet with you." Amy cupped the phone between her shoulder and chin, reached for a note pad and scribbled across the page. "Monday the fourteenth. We have you down. Thank you."

Amy made an excited face and hung up.

"I had no idea I had my very own in-house emoji," Jill said.

Amy clapped her hands together, then lifted them to her lips. "You will not believe who that was on the phone. Liz Fuller, the buyer for Sloan's. She wants to talk with you about designing their back-to-school line for teen girls."

"Oh, my gosh." Jill shot from her chair. "That's less than a year from now."

Jill had waited for an opportunity like this since she'd moved to New York. This should have been one of the most exciting moments in her business life, but the Eagle Eye article not only cast a shadow on the moment, but on her character. If anyone figured out she was the teen designer in question she'd be ruined.

"She'll be here next week if you're available," Amy said.

"I'm available."

"See. Already things are looking up."

"Either that or she doesn't read the *Post*."

CHAPTER EIGHT

Jill left the brownstone and headed for the subway. It had been a week since the article and not one cancellation as a result. Every time the phone rang Jill and Amy held their breath that it wasn't Sloan's buyer calling to cancel. Still too soon to disregard the article's possible influence, but as days passed with no repercussions she and Amy breathed a sigh of relief at the end of each closing day.

Remarkably during this time, JJ Designs acquired two new accounts. Small, but legitimate, none-the-less.

The only good thing about the article was it had forced her to stop obsessing about Phil. As a result, her focus and energy had been absorbed by the Sloan's account.

Liz Fuller had loved her preliminary sketches for the back-to-school line and had scheduled a follow-up in early February for the mock-ups. That gave her two months to make the proto-types. If Liz liked them, then a contract would soon follow. But there was much work to be done before that became a possibility, much less a reality.

In thirty minutes she had a meeting with LNO's founder, Anna Delany and a freelance reporter regarding an article for the Like No Other Foundation. But first, she had to stop by her office before the meeting to check that all was on schedule with the girls in the sewing room.

After exiting the subway station, she walked the half block to her building. She crossed the foyer just as the elevator started to close. She hurried forward. "Hold the door!"

As she ran across the marble floor, a masculine hand slipped between the doors popping them apart. The elevator opened to a tall, well-dressed man standing to one side. She caught a subtle whiff of citrus and spice reminding her of a blue-eyed, bearded street guy. The scent wasn't quite the same as his, but there was something familiar about it. She inhaled deeply, but the scent had disappeared. Just like him.

As she stepped through the opening she glanced at the man's face. He stood staring at her, lips parted as if he was about to speak. But, then he blinked and abruptly turned his gaze to the number panel in front of him.

Jill wondered if he'd thought he knew her from somewhere. That type of thing was fairly common in the city. Everybody seemed to look like someone else.

She cut her eyes in his direction. The man seemed inordinately preoccupied with the numbers slowly clicking above the door. His dark hair was cut in a short, trendy style and he was clean-shaven. Talk about gorgeous. It was nice to *finally* have an effect on someone older than seventeen. She glanced down at her navy slacks and caramel sweater and smothered a smile. Maybe she should dress less like a teenager more often.

She couldn't help herself and eased her head slowly to the right hoping for another glimpse of the gentleman's face. Except for that first glance when she'd stepped into the elevator, all she could see now was his profile. Which told her very little as he stared at the glowing numbers overhead. Same height and hair color as Phil, but that didn't mean a thing. Lots of six-foot-two, dark-haired, hot guys on the planet.

Sighing, she lifted her gaze to the scrolling numbers, wondering why people became so interested in them once on an elevator. She glanced several times between the pokey numbers and his profile.

"Slow, isn't it?" she said. "The building only has eight stories, but at times feels more like eighty."

He nodded and continued staring ahead.

Come on. Look at me.

"Hope you're not in a hurry," she said.

"Not at all."

"Just visiting?"

"Yes." The man glanced at his wristwatch, checked the time, then planted his gaze onto the elevator control panel.

Jill ran her glance over his dark navy suit. Tropical wool. Definitely tailored. Fit too well not to be. Exactly the kind of suit she'd envisioned for her homeless guy. *There I go again.*

"Isn't it funny how people get on an elevator and mindlessly stare at the numbers?" She smiled, but her attempt to engage him fell flat.

"Maybe that someone doesn't want to be disturbed."

"Oh." She shrugged. "I guess not." Silence and number watching. "I suppose it *is* awkward. I mean, why would perfect strangers want to start a conversation that's doomed from the first word. How much can one *really* say between floors? Of any substance, that is."

She glanced back at him and found him staring at her, wearing the most delightfully confused expression she'd ever seen on a man.

"I'm sorry." She grinned. "I *am* disturbing you. I'll shut up."

The elevator dinged and the doors slid open on seven. Jill stepped off at her floor. Still curious about the man, she glanced back. Just as the doors started to close she caught the glimmer of a smile on the stranger's face. He was still looking up at the numbers.

*　*　*

Jill's heels clicked against the tile floor as she headed down the corridor to her office suite. "Guess I didn't disturb him too much."

JJ Designs scrolled in a glossy-white script across the door of her company. She unlocked it, then stepped through the doorway. After turning on the entry light, she plugged in the Christmas tree lights. Then proceeded throughout the suite, flicking on hall and break-room lights.

On her way to her office, she stopped at Amy's desk to leave a few notes regarding the floral tops in her spring line. That done, she glanced at her watch. Almost nine. Before heading out, she ducked into the sewing room to pair the fabric with the correct patterns for production. Satisfied, she left the office.

Moments later she pushed through the door of Like No Other Foundation. As soon as she entered, she stopped. The stranger from the elevator sat on a white chair and held a yellow mug to his lips.

"So this is where you were going."

The man shot to his feet, coughing uncontrollably, and sloshed hot coffee onto his pant leg.

"Blast it!" He wheezed and coughed again.

"I'm so sorry." Jill hurried over to him. "I didn't mean to startle you."

He lifted his hand, his mouth set in annoyance. "It's all right." Clearing his throat, he quickly set down his mug and brushed the excess liquid with the back of his hand.

Jill dove for a nearby tissue box, snatched out a wad, then furiously began pressing it against the wet fabric. Between dabs she glanced up at him, her mind twisting into a swirl of delightful knots. To say he was *put out* with her was an understatement. Even in anger he was gorgeous. Coffee, mingled with grapefruit and spice tingled her senses. As if he'd recently stepped from a fresh rain shower, or the—

"Really." The man grabbed her wrist and pulled her to her feet. "It's okay."

She straightened, glad to see his glare had turned more to a slight frown. Somewhat relieved, she stepped back and tossed the tissue into the trash. "Tropical wool. I think it'll be fine. Dry cleaning should take care of it. The good news is you didn't use cream."

"Thank you." He grimaced. "I feel much better knowing that."

Well, excuse me. "Grouch." She spoke under her breath just as Annie entered the room.

"Cameron, I see you've met Jill."

"Yes, we have," he said. "But I fear your friend has caught me in a *grouchy* mood."

"I'm sorry?" Annie glanced at him clearly confused.

Jill pursed her lips and slanted her gaze in his direction. But it seemed he only had eyes for Annie.

"It's nothing." Cam waved his right hand in the air. "We've just been discussing the merits of dry cleaning." He cocked a dark brow in Jill's direction and smiled.

Jill felt the need to add, "I startled him when I came in and he spilled coffee on his pants."

"Oh, I see. Well." She clapped her hands together. "Sit down. Both of you."

They each took a seat on the white, leather club chairs and Annie parked herself on the sofa opposite.

"Jill, first of all, I heard about the pending offer from Sloan's. Congratulations."

"Thank you. It's not a done deal, yet…but I'm really excited about it." Smiling, she turned to Cameron, but all she got from him was a sardonic glance. She sobered and gave her attention back to Annie.

"And Cameron, I want to thank you for agreeing to do a story for my foundation."

"My pleasure."

"I'm sure you're both wondering why I wanted you two to meet." She turned her attention to Cameron. "After you interview me, I'd like for you to tag Jill for the next couple of weeks or so. You'll get to see first-hand the ins and outs of how we do things. Jill Jeffrey has her own line of clothing for teenage girls and is LNO's latest ambassador. Jill and I have done several workshops together and she does amazing work with these young women. As a matter of fact, she's one of several we're considering for our board."

Jill fluttered an appropriate smile. But the last thing she wanted was to have a journalist tag after her.

Annie glanced between her two listeners, smiling pointedly at Jill. "The girls absolutely adore her. And Cameron, I thought since fashion week was next month this would be a great plug for JJ Designs, as well. Think you could pull that off?" She smiled.

Cameron flicked his blue-eyed gaze in Jill's direction giving her the once over before coming back to linger on her face. "I think I can find a way to tie the two together."

Jill's breath caught in her throat. She had the sudden impulse to get up and run. What the heck was his problem? Maybe she was being overly sensitive, but something about his appraisal stung. The thought of spending an entire two weeks in this man's company didn't sit well with her.

Jill sighed inwardly. LNO was hanging on by a thread. If their donations didn't improve Annie was going to have to shut down the foundation. She'd just have to make the best of it.

"What do you think, Jill? Promoting your fresh, trendy, teen fashions is the least I can do to thank you for all your volunteer work."

Silence filled the room until she realized Annie was waiting for her response.

"Oh, gosh." Jill spread her hands wide. "You know how much I appreciate your generosity, but please, no. I don't want the story to be about me, not in any way. I mean—"

"Nonsense, it's all part of the package," Annie said. "And I want the world beyond New York to know about you."

"I think that's a great idea." Cam lifted his hand and spanned it across the space in front of them like a byline to a front-page story. "Up and coming teen fashion sensation takes time from her busy schedule to give to those *less fortunate*."

Jill gaped at him. His tone and words did not mix, nor did they sit well with her.

"I like it," Annie said. "Human interest meets philanthropy. But Cameron, it's not just the less fortunate we work with. LNO works with teen girls from all demographics. Why, last spring, Jill worked with a group of debutants."

"And I'm sure she fit in quite well with them," he said.

Cam gazed at Jill as if he were daring her to disagree. Then it hit her…this man did not like her…from his rudeness on the elevator, to his chilly reception of her now. Oh, no. The article. Could Cameron have read it and already put two and two together, assuming Eagle Eye was referring to her?

She thought of that despicable man who'd written the piece on New York's homeless. What had he called her? *User. Sensationalist. Manipulator.* His words spilled across her brain, just as hurtful as when she'd first read them.

She eyed the man seated next to her and gave him look for look. She had news for Mr. Phillips. She didn't like his kind either. He and that Eagle were undoubtedly cut from the same cloth. The sooner she could get this over with, the better. She wondered if he knew The Eagle. The same way she knew the names of her competition, journalists probably had their own little club as well.

Mmm. Maybe a couple of weeks in Cameron Phillips' company would turn out to her benefit and not just that of Like No Other.

* * *

Cameron had barely gotten over his surprise at being in such close proximity in the elevator, when Jill strolled into LNO's office ten minutes later like a petite whirlwind. Lively and utterly charming. Just like the night he'd met her on the street corner.

Anger churned in his gut, and he wasn't sure if it was at her or himself. At the last minute, Annie had sent a text saying she'd invited a designer friend to join them, but failed to mention the designer's name. Seems Miss Jeffrey got around, which shouldn't have surprised him. He'd bet his next paycheck the Jeffrey millions were somehow involved. Either way, there was little doubt money changed hands.

He thought of the check for twenty grand that had tumbled from her purse. In the underground, Jill had assured *Phil* the money was for charity, but that didn't mean she hadn't had another motive in mind. From his point of view it now looked more like payment for a coveted board position.

She'd admitted to tracking him down. And her apology? Was that even genuine, or simply to clear her conscience?

Something had stirred in his mid-section while she'd chatted about removing the coffee stain from his pants. Then she'd gazed up at him, her honest brown eyes filled with an innocent expectancy he still found extremely appealing. As if her explanation had solved his problem, she'd stood waiting for his reply, gazing at him with the same candor as the night she'd approached him outside the Plaza Hotel.

Truthfully, he'd been drawn to her open, "I have nothing to hide" expression, even then. Too bad it was simply a ruse to catch unsuspecting men off their guard. But, damned if he still wasn't attracted to the ruse *and* to her.

When Jill had gazed so intently up at him, he'd feared she might recognize him. He'd held his breath waiting for the moment. But the moment hadn't come. She'd had no idea who he was and he'd planned to keep it that way. He'd have his meeting with the founder of Like No Other, interview her for his story, then be on his way. Putting as much space between him and little Miss Jeffrey as New York City would allow.

Thankfully, just as he was about to speak, Annie had walked in interrupting the moment. Good thing, too. Even though it was unlikely she'd identify him by his voice, the less he said to her the better. But, that dream was short lived.

Annie's proposal he shadow Jill, almost had him wishing he'd stayed in bed that morning. The thought of having to *pretend* with this young woman for two entire weeks didn't sit well with his sense of right and wrong. Honesty was one virtue he was happy to say he owned, but instead of using his way with words to get out of the situation, he'd used them to seal the deal. More fool him. The fact Jill hadn't recognized him or his voice during this meeting was a good sign and made it unlikely she'd be able to in the future. So for the time being he could rest easy.

"I hate to rush our meeting, but now that I have you two settled," Annie glanced over at Cam, "I'd like to get on with our interview if that's okay. I have an early flight in the morning and have a million things to get done before then."

"Of course. Let's get started." He glanced at Jill hoping she'd leave.

As if she could read his thoughts, she stood. "I'll leave you both to it, then." She turned toward Cameron. "It was nice meeting you."

"Here's my card," he said. "Let me know your schedule and we'll set something up."

"Of course." Jill hugged Annie, then left.

Cam struggled within. The sooner he interviewed Annie, the sooner he could focus on a plan to get through the next two weeks.

* * *

Jill had taken Cameron's cell number with the promise to call the next day or so. When she arrived back in her office, Amy met her at the door with a long face.

"What is it?"

"It's The Lady Bug. They've cancelled the order for the floral blouses."

Jill's heart sank. "Why? Was it the fabric?"

"They asked me point blank if the teen designer mentioned in The Eagle Eye article was you."

Heat fast-flushed over her entire body.

"Of course I told them it wasn't," Amy said.

Jill stepped to her desk chair and sank down.

"Then the Rep mentioned the gala and said she was there herself and knew for a fact you were the only teen designer present. So, who else could it be, except you?"

"Well, at least The Lady Bug only wanted a small order. It could be worse, right?"

Amy slouched down in the chair opposite Jill's. "She *could* start telling others in the industry." Dejected, they both stared at the floor.

"I can't believe this is happening." Jill pressed fingers to her temple. "This is so unfair."

"You know what I think? I think you should write a response in the opinion section."

"And say what? That it wasn't me, when it was?"

"But this is not the way it happened. He doesn't even list details."

Jill picked up the article. A photo of a bald eagle's head was to the right of author's pen name, Eagle Eye. The tag line, *Watching Out for You*, scrolled in bold black ink underneath.

A swarm of butterflies churned in the pit of her stomach. "We have to face it, Amy. It's only a matter of time before everyone in the district finds out it's me."

CHAPTER NINE

Jill sat at her desk twirling a strand of her hair around her finger. "Amy, do you think we should get out more?"

Amy stopped wrapping her scarf around her neck and stared at her. "Speak for yourself, I get out plenty."

"Oh, I know. I guess, I'm really talking about me."

"You do spend a lot of evenings here working. You *should* go out and have some fun."

"You're absolutely right." Jill lifted her coat off the wall hook and followed Amy to the entrance. A few minutes later they exited the building.

"If you don't have any plans this evening, why don't we check out Flora Bar?"

"I'm sorry." Amy stuck a finger in her right ear and jiggled. "Did you say *bar*?"

"Ha, ha. It's a restaurant. But, I'm sure they also have a nice bar if that's what you'd like."

"I know what it is. Pricy place. A bit out of our league. What's gotten into you?"

"Nothing." Jill shrugged. "Can't a couple of girls sit at a bar?"

"An expensive bar. And according to you, no bar is nice, even the high-priced ones."

"That was the old me. So, come on. Do you want to go?"

"I can't tonight." Amy pulled a sad face. "I have a date. I'm sorry."

"Since when?"

"Since…you know, when you told me it was okay to like a particular person."

"You're going out with Mark?"

"Yeeesss."

"Oh."

"You're hurt."

"No. I'm not. Don't even think that."

Amy glanced at the sidewalk and tugged her scarf tightly around her neck.

"I'm just surprised, that's all," Jill said. "Who would've thought with all that sparring between the two of you…"

"I guess what they say is true. Hate is akin to love."

"I guess."

"Rain check?"

"Sure."

Amy went left to catch the subway, while Jill turned right, heading to the corner. She flagged a taxi. "Flora Bar, please. Upper East Side. Madison Avenue."

The subterranean room sported high ceilings and massive windows that overlooked a lovely courtyard. Jill opted to sit at the bar, as the tables were all reserved.

"This isn't so bad." She hung her coat over her seat back, then sat down.

A young woman handed Jill a menu and poured her a glass of water. "The day's specials are on this card and the wine list is on the back. Can I get you something else to drink while you look over the menu?"

"I'll have a club soda with orange juice and a twist of lime, please."

While she waited for her drink, she perused the menu. Seafood sounded good. Her eye focused on the platter dish. One hundred and forty dollars. Yikes! Maybe not. She settled on the lobster ravioli at thirty dollars, instead.

Jill had just raised her club soda to her lips when she heard a familiar voice behind her.

"May I join you?"

Jill swiveled in her seat.

Cameron Phillips stood, one hand on the back of the bar seat next to her, his penetrating gaze all but demanding a yes.

"Ah, sure." Actually she wasn't at all sure, but what else could she say. Her two weeks may as well start now. She took a sip of her drink, set the glass on the bar counter and turned to him. He had taken the seat and was already placing his order.

"I'll try the seafood platter," he said. "And a Bud Lite."

"Watching your figure?" She couldn't resist asking and received a crooked smile in response.

"One has to start somewhere."

She liked the way one side of his mouth lifted in a half smile. Cameron Phillips... To say he was good looking was an understatement. She'd fought her attraction to him ever since his rudeness in Annie's office. On the surface, he was the best looking man she'd ever seen, but the inner man, well, that had yet to be determined. One thing was certain, his close proximity sent a million flurries to her mid-section. To still the flutters, she placed her hand against her stomach.

"You feeling okay?"

"Um, yes." She quickly removed her hand and took hold of her glass. He was way too observant. "So do you come here often?" she asked.

"As a matter of fact I do. And you?"

"This is my first time."

"Forgive me for saying so, but I didn't figure you as the *sit alone at a bar* type."

"I'm not usually, but someone recently told me that I and my friends needed to get out more."

A telling twinkle appeared in his eyes, making her treacherous heart leap in her throat. The delightful near-smile hovering about his firm lips didn't help matters, either. She wondered what could be so funny.

He made a point of looking around. "I don't see any friends."

"I invited my assistant, but she already had other plans."

"So you braved the masses and came by yourself."

At that moment, the waitress delivered each of their meals, refilled their water glasses, then left.

"As you'll soon discover, Mr. Phillips, it takes more than mere mortals to scare me."

* * *

No truer words were ever spoken. The places she frequented alone would give most men pause. But, not her.

She forked a generous portion of ravioli and shoved it in her mouth. As she chewed, she glanced at him, swallowed, then quickly grabbed her drink. She seemed nervous. Until this moment, he hadn't thought of her as the nervous type, either.

"How's your pasta?"

"Delicious." She eyed his sizeable platter. "How's your dinner? It looks amazing."

"It is. I get this every time I come here. It's one of Flora Bar's specialties. You should try it sometime."

"I'll be sure to do that, after my first million."

He'd assumed she'd come from a wealthy family, but maybe that's all it was, an assumption on his part. If she was all about making it on her own, then he respected that.

"It is pricy, I admit. But I believe one should enjoy the occasional luxury. Life's too short not to."

"Spoken like a man who has little to no responsibilities."

"And you do?"

She paused, fork mid-air. "And how many people are on your payroll?"

"Touché. If you don't mind my asking, how many are on yours?" he said.

"Five, including me." She took a sip of water. "Admittedly, three are only part-time, but still…"

"You're to be commended. I don't know many twenty-five-year-olds who've come close to what you've accomplished."

"How do you know I'm twenty-five?"

He couldn't very well tell her he'd seen her driver's license. He shrugged. "A lucky guess on my part."

"And I'd say you're twenty-nine? Thirty?"

"Thirty-two."

Jill went back to concentrating on her dinner. In other words, *shut the heck up, Cameron*.

As Cam forked the creamy coleslaw, he thought about her earlier comment. He was fairly certain it was *Phil's* reference to 'getting out more' that she'd referred to. He marveled at her obsession with him. What was it about *Phil* that affected her so? Something drove her and he wouldn't be an investigative reporter worth his salt if he didn't try to discover why. Maybe something would come to light over the next couple of weeks in her company.

She broke off a crusty piece of bread and buttered it. She had the prettiest hands. The pink polish on her nails reminded him of vender's tulips sold along the city sidewalks in the spring.

As much as he'd like to, he couldn't deny his growing attraction to her. He'd be lying if he did. From that first moment near the Plaza, Jill had gotten under his skin and he wasn't at all happy about that. Did she really think she could hide her true motives behind her wide-eyed innocence and adorable charm? No man liked to be duped.

He liked being in control and the fact that fate had flung them together irritated him. On the one hand, he'd wanted nothing to do with her, but her obsession with Phil both fascinated and perplexed him. Who she was with Phil didn't sync with who she was with Cameron. With Cameron, she was tentative and suspicious. Irritated and snarky. But with Phil she seemed more honest and caring. Open and frank.

When they were on the elevator together, she was charm itself. Doing her best to strike up a conversation with him. Then it hit him. It was not until after she discovered his occupation that she became standoffish. And if he were honest, he wasn't the nicest guy either, in the elevator, or at Annie's.

He'd just have to let things play out. So far, that stunt she'd pulled at the gala outweighed any romantic feelings he may have had at first.

CHAPTER TEN

Saturday afternoon Cameron had run late joining Jill at Johnson Middle School. He wished he could have said no to Annie's request to shadow her, but it would have seemed more than odd to Annie in light of her connection with Ethan Knight. At least he could use his time with Jill for one or more fluff articles. And if he could tie in Annie's work with the less fortunate in society, it might fit well with some of his future pieces.

The principal escorted him to the classroom where the second workshop was in full swing. He thanked the woman and quietly took a chair in the back of the room.

He caught Jill's eye, giving her a brief nod. After he slipped his reporter's notebook from his breast pocket, he settled back to observe and take notes, which would later serve as the basis for his interview questions. He only needed a flavor of the session and could get the other details from Jill during his interview.

Jill Jeffrey literally performed at the front of the room. As he watched her, he had to admit, she was certainly in her element. Completely animated and utterly charming, she had each girl under her spell. As she talked, their eyes never left her face. They hung on her every word. Giggled at her jokes, and groaned at the corny ones.

Jill's diminutive form and choice of dress made her *look* every bit the teenager. She was one of them. Her dark head came a bit lower than the tallest girl in the room. She had to go up on tiptoe when she pointed to the oversized fashion chart, nearly knocking it over at one point in her presentation. But, her knowledge of the subject, her confidence and stage presence told a different story.

"Mixing and matching is key to a basic wardrobe," she said. "You don't need a million pieces of clothing to look great or to have what you need for most occasions."

"What about prom?" the tall brunette said.

"That's a specialty item, Terri, and totally necessary, of course."

"Along with heels and some bling," a short blonde added.

"Of course, Shelley, bling is absolutely essential. And a purchase like that needs to be done earlier than later. For example, you can buy your prom dress the summer before while they're on sale. Or, if you sew or know someone who does, that's another way to manage your budget. Plus you'll have an original creation to wear." Jill's generous smile radiated across the small group.

"Okay. Next Saturday, we're meeting in the Home Ec room to try our hand at a bit of sewing. I'll have a special surprise for you, so I hope you all can make it. Have a great weekend, everybody."

The scraping of metal chairs against tile and a flurry of female chatter filled the classroom. Cameron stood and waited for the girls to exit, then meandered over to Jill who was in the process of taking down the poster.

"Here. Let me help with that."

"It's okay, I've got it."

With the poster tucked underneath her arm, she turned toward him. "So what did you think?"

"I think you did a nice job. I don't know much about teenage girls, but they seemed enamored with you."

"You say that like it's a bad thing."

"Not at all. You're a rock star."

"Hardly, I'm just one of them and they see that. I'm real with them."

"And honest?"

She paused and looked pointedly at him. "Yes. I am."

He thought about how she'd used him in some frivolous bet. For the evening's entertainment. He'd met many like her before. Entitled. Spoiled. Not caring who they hurt for a lark. Like many of them, Jill hid her real motives behind sparkling conversation and charm. So what if she was doing a good deed for these kids. Well, time would tell what her motives really were.

"Good. They need someone to be honest with them." Cam said.

They made their way down the hallway to the exit.

"You say that like you may know something about it."

"Let's just say as a journalist, I've had my share of experiences with the less fortunate."

"I see." She gazed at him with the same inquisitive expression she'd had the first time they'd met. Waiting for more. As if she were really interested.

He brushed his fingers across his chin. "Let me at least help you to the car with this stuff, then let's grab dinner. I'd like to interview you if you're free."

She glanced at her wristwatch. "Um...sure."

She was hesitant. It was obvious she didn't want to go with him any more than he wanted to shadow her. He knew what his issues were, but what were hers?

* * *

They settled in a booth at Nathan's deli on Fifty-Seventh Street. The local restaurant famous for their hot dogs was usually crowded and noisy, but most of the diners were already at the

Knicks game so the place was practically deserted. They each ordered a loaded foot-long hot dog with fries.

"I see you're a young woman with an appetite. You certainly polished off that ravioli last night."

"Is that a bad thing?"

"No. Not at all. It's actually nice to eat with someone who prefers a meal with substance. I find most fashion-conscious women something more in the line of Brussels sprouts and quinoa."

"It's pronounced, 'keen wah.' If you're going to say it at least get it right."

"You've just made my point." He wrapped his fingers around the messy hotdog and lifted it to his mouth.

"Hey, with my height, I have to eat healthy most of the time. Trust me, this decadent mass of deliciousness is a rare treat."

"I agree. *Bon appétit.*"

"Well, now that we have that established… What would you like to know?"

He dabbed a napkin to his mouth. "How long have you been working with LNO?"

"Not that long. About a year and a half. I met Annie on the elevator one afternoon almost two years ago. She was on her way to work with *her girls*, as she likes to call them. She asked if I wanted to join her. I said, sure, and she said, 'We'll have to get permission from your mother.' I burst out laughing, then informed her I was twenty-three."

He couldn't help but smile. He'd assumed the same thing the first time he'd met her.

"In her defense, I'd no makeup on and because of my height people often mistake me for a much younger person."

He nodded. "I can see how that would happen. So, you went with her."

"Yes. The meeting was much like the one today, only much shorter."

"Why? What determines the length?"

"Time, facility space. Most of LNO's workshops take place on four Saturdays over the course of a month. Anyway, that day the girls were from a children's home. Most of them were around fourteen years old. The session was *less is more*."

"Which means…" He jotted a few notes as Jill explained.

"Oh, you know, less makeup on the face, allowing their own natural glow to shine through." She fisted her hands underneath her chin and propped her elbows on the table. "Except for the occasional break-out, most teenage girls don't realize how flawless their skin really is. They're so unsure of themselves. Think about it, these young women are competing with celebrities that are *way* overly made up for magazine ads, TV, and movies."

He glanced up from his long skinny tablet. "What else?"

"Um, fewer clothes in the closet. Learning to layer items and mix and match. There are basics to a woman's wardrobe and they don't have to be expensive. Most, if not all of the latest fashion trends can be found at discount stores. Annie knows many of these girls have very little in the way of material things, so her goal is to teach them the basics of any wardrobe and makeup drawer. Her philosophy being, frugal is smart. Less, means less clutter, corners that breathe, less to have to think about, which allows more time for what's truly important in life."

He gazed at Jill's animated features. She'd lit up like the Fourth of July. Bursting with information and passion. She loved what she was doing and it was obvious she cared about these girls. Had a real heart for them, no matter what their status. Her enthusiasm for LNO didn't jive with what she'd done to him six weeks ago. Had he misjudged her? He thought about the article and that one little paragraph lampooning her. Remorse dinged his conscience, but he pushed it aside.

At this moment he was thankful he'd deleted Jill's name from the story. And frankly, he wished he'd never even referred to her. How was he supposed to have known he'd ever see her again much less be asked to work with her?

And since when did withholding the truth become the criteria for a journalist?

Never.

He'd done the right thing. But somehow that didn't make him feel any better.

He set the pen aside, sat back and locked his gaze on her heart-shaped face. "What's important to Jill Jeffrey?"

"Right now," she shrugged a slender shoulder, "business success, for one. I've worked long hours to make JJ Designs what it is today. Every penny I make I put right back into my company. I want it to grow, to become nationally known."

"And internationally?"

"I wouldn't say no to that." She leaned forward, a twinkle in her eye. "Ultimately, what I really want is my own line of boutiques, similar to Lilly Bette's, but mine will be a one-stop shopping experience for what every teenage girl needs. I'll design clothes for every occasion. From school outfits to coats, prom dresses to debutant gowns. I'll contract with other designers for shoes, purses, jewelry, hair accessories and even makeup."

"Big dreams for such a little girl."

"I may be small in stature, but not so in other areas of my life." She sat back and looked a bit deflated by his comment.

He nodded. "I learned from my interview with Annie, LNO's fundraising is down. Apparently, her supposed involvement with Alex Langdon still troubles some."

"I know." Jill nodded. "She also shared some of that with me. I'm hoping to help more with that side of things. Even though Alex is in jail, I guess it'll take some time before people trust the organization again."

"There's definitely some truth to that." He thought about his own trust issues with Jill. Speaking of trust, she still seemed a bit reserved with him. Not at all, the wide-eyed trusting young woman he'd met weeks ago. Of course, she'd been playing some sort of game at the time—to maneuver him inside for the sake of the bet.

"Let's hope nothing else has happened that could add suspicion to the foundation." Cam watched for her reaction.

Jill's eyes widened ever so slightly. Suddenly guarded, her face grew noticeably pale. She swirled a French fry into a glob of ketchup. "Let's hope not."

"Well, I think that's all the questions I have for now."

Jill nodded and quickly reached for her handbag.

"This is my treat," he said.

"Thanks."

He paid the waiter and slid from the booth. "May I see you home?"

"No, thank you." She took her oversized tote from him and slipped it on her shoulder. "Next Saturday I'm finishing up today's group with something special. You're welcome to come if you'd like."

"That's right. You mentioned that in your closing remarks. What's the surprise?"

"I'm creating a pattern just for them."

"A pattern?"

"A simple A-line dress. Something they'll all be able to make."

"I see."

"If that doesn't fit your schedule, I'm also starting up another group that same day. It's in the afternoon, if you care to stop by. It's at Billings Community Center, in Queens. Two o'clock."

"Sure, but per Annie's wishes, I'd like to shadow you at work if I may."

Jill hesitated. "Um, sure. My offices are one floor below LNO's suite. Seventh floor, JJ Designs, number twelve. I'm in the office all week. We start around 9:00 a.m. Feel free to come any time after that."

"I will."

Chapter Eleven

Monday morning, Jill continued to ponder Cameron's disturbing comment at Nathan's Hot Dogs. Her actions could most certainly add suspicion to LNO if anyone discovered the teen fashion designer in question was her. A wave of sickness fluttered her mid-section. Time alone would tell. Each day's passing without incident made it less and less likely anything would ever come of the article. But that wouldn't make the days that followed any less stressful. Both she and Amy were fully aware of the consequences should Jill be identified as the *manipulator of the homeless*.

She put the last of her blouse drawings for The Lady Bug boutique into a folder to be filed. The blouses were some of her favorite designs and unless another trendy boutique wanted them, they'd remain under lock and key. She hated to lose this client, having had high hopes for a long-term relationship with them. But at least the designs were still hers. That was most important.

Jill opened her laptop and typed, *Can a pseudonym keep you anonymous online,* in the search engine.

"Can a pseudonym protect your privacy? Take for example Michael… A temporary privacy…connection to…online activity." Jill leaned back in her desk chair. "This is not at all helpful."

She continued to read hoping to find one clue that might lead her in discovering Eagle Eye's real identity. She clicked on another site. "Here's something… Fake name is not the same as anonymity. Each word you write under that name, gives a reader a clue to that person's identity."

She grabbed the article from the desk side drawer. Starting at the first word, she slowly re-read the expose'. Knots formed in her stomach, tightening with each sentence she read. "There had to be a clue to who this person was. One word, a turn of phrase, something."

Amy stuck her head in the doorway. "Jill, Cameron Phillips is here."

"Be right there." Jill folded the newspaper, laid it aside, and stood.

Jill found Cameron hovering over the shoulder of Kelley Martin, one of her seamstresses, in the main design room. He looked up when she entered.

"Hi, Cameron."

"Please call me Cam."

She smiled and nodded.

"You have quite a place here," he said. "Kelley was just showing me a little bit of the process."

"My pleasure, Mr. Phillips."

"It's still small by most standards, but we get by." Jill ran her gaze over Cameron's outfit.

"What?" He glanced downward. "Something not to your liking?"

"Oh, no. You look great. I just have this habit of noticing what people wear." *Plus you have a habit of looking right through me and perusing your clothes seemed less threatening.* "So, how about I continue with the tour?"

"Lead the way."

"As you can see our studio is open for the most part, with a few places carved out for privacy when needed. My office, which is behind me, doesn't have an actual door, but simply opens to the main room. Tucking it in the corner is sufficient for my needs.

"For the longest time, I was a one woman show, then Amy came onboard and between the two of us we managed to produce some wonderful designs."

"And now you're five."

"Right. Five counting me."

"What's down the hallway?"

"The kitchen, a storage closet, and a bathroom, including a shower and a tub."

"I can see having the shower, but a tub? Seems a bit overkill."

"Not if I want to dye a fabric. A sink is way too small for that. And then there's the occasional need for an enzyme wash and that's why I have a washing machine here. In case you wanted to know."

The corner of his mouth lifted in a half-smile. "I see."

"Otherwise, all the magic goes on right here." She stopped mid-stride in the center of the rectangular workroom.

"What's happening over there?" Cam nodded toward a long rectangular table covered in a mass of color where two young women painstakingly bent over their task.

"They're securing the fabric to the pattern, then they'll cut it out. Simple really. The sewing machines are along that far wall, as you can see."

"What are those?" He pointed to the small metal objects being placed along the edge of one pattern.

"Weights. Sometimes they're easier to use than the pins. It's simply a personal preference."

"I see."

"Let's head to the kitchen and grab a coffee, then we can chat in my office if you'd like."

* * *

Cam sat down in one of two spare chairs in Jill's office while she took the one behind the large table-like desk in the center of the room. Glass jars filled with hundreds of colored pencils hugged the corners. Bins of buttons and notions were stacked along one wall of cubbies. Pencil drawings of everything from dresses to leggings covered the wall behind her desk. Some were framed and others merely pinned to the sheetrock. Every corner of her space held clutter and he wondered how anyone could accomplish anything of significance here. The mass of color and fabrics had a dizzying effect and he glanced away.

"Sorry for the mess." It was as if she knew what he was thinking. As she spoke she gathered and stacked pages of drawings and strewn pencils, quickly shoving them to one side. She looked right at him. "I just hope I can find it all after you leave." She took a sip of her coffee. "So, how do you know Annie?"

"She and I have a mutual friend, Ethan Knight—the owner of Apalacha Key, Florida's local paper. I'm seriously thinking about investing in it. Ethan's actually the one who suggested I write this article for Annie."

"How nice." She laced her fingers around her coffee mug and waited for him to continue.

It was now his turn. She was not going to offer any more.

"Look, it's obvious you don't want me here. Is it me or is it simply journalists in general you find distasteful?"

Her gaze dropped from his. "How astute of you to notice."

"It's part of the job." The words hadn't left his mouth when he glimpsed the edge of the *New York Post* tucked among the mass of paper near her elbow. His heart stopped. She knew about the article.

"It seems I've given you the impression that I don't like reporters. But," she shrugged. "I don't like reporters. At the moment, there's one in particular who lacks both scruples and conscience."

"So, because of this one person, you're painting all of us with the same broad brush?"

Jill stared at him as if trying to digest what he'd just said.

He thought of the *Post* article mere inches away. His *hit* piece, as he'd heard it described through the grapevine. Was it any wonder she didn't trust him? He was a reporter. And because of that he was the enemy.

"Maybe it would help if you think of me as simply doing a favor for Annie."

She glanced at her coffee, then back at him. "Truthfully, that doesn't help. And I think it's a mistake to link my design company with Like No Other. I'm happy to have you tag me when I'm working with the foundation and you're welcome to interview the girls, if they and their parents don't object, but my design studio is not important to the story."

"Annie seems to think otherwise."

"Annie is being generous. That's who she is. She's a very giving person."

"And you? Are you a giving person?"

"I think so, yes. But your tone and the fact that you had to ask, tells me otherwise."

She was right. He did question her motives. And her astuteness on the matter should not have surprised him. He had accused her of painting with a broad brush, but wasn't that exactly what he'd done? Putting her in the same category as the other social climbers he'd known and unfortunately, in one particular instance, loved?

This young woman was not the childlike, doe-eyed creature from the charity gala, simply out for a lark. There was more to her than he'd first thought. He couldn't deny his growing interest in discovering who she really was beneath that teenage facade. One thing was certain. He'd hurt her with that article. As a result, the open, hopeful young woman from the gala had disappeared. "I'm sorry. That wasn't my intent," he said.

"While we're being so forthcoming, I have a question for you."

"Go ahead."

"You seem rather aloof when you're with me. Why is that?"

"I do?"

"Yes. You avoid eye contact for one. Your answers to my questions are short and to the point as if you're hiding something." She paused. "Am I right?"

He'd have to tread carefully here.

"And yours haven't been?"

She huffed out a breath.

"I must confess I did have a preconceived opinion about you or I should say, your type," he said.

"My type?"

"The type where social status is everything."

A combination of pain and disbelief filled her eyes.

"When have I ever given you that impression? I mean… you've disliked me from the first day we met, in Annie's office. You didn't even know me and yet you formed such an opinion?"

"You're right. That was wrong of me. I realize that now. It's just that you reminded me of someone who has—let's just say, lost my trust."

"Good grief. You sound like some of the teenage girls I work with."

He burst out laughing. "I do, don't I?"

For a moment she just sat there glaring at him. Then a glimmer of a smile played about her pink lips. "I guess we've both been guilty of painting with too big a brush."

Jill glanced at the cup of coffee in her hand and took a hasty sip. "I love working with teenage girls. I guess Annie and I have a similar heart when it comes to them. You can put that in your article."

"Are you considering her board position?"

"Sure, I'd be crazy not to. But there are two other people in the running."

"You do know being on a board is synonymous with fundraising. Have you done much?" He lifted his hand to his mouth and watched her.

"Only once. It's a great deal of work as you can imagine."

"And did you learn anything helpful in the process?"

"That one has to have more than talent to make a success of it. Many times it comes down to who you know."

"That's true." He imagined the opportunity to be on LNO's board and to work with an internationally known fashion icon was too good to pass up.

"At this time in my life, I don't have the resources to give money myself. I put most of what I make back into my business. Someday, if I'm successful, I hope I'm able to give more. But until then, all I have to give is time and a bit of expertise."

She opened her hands and shrugged. "And yes, fundraising is important to a charity." She shook her head. "I'm certainly not of the same caliber as the rest of her board. Before I accept any position with them I'll have to make it clear what I can realistically commit to. I'm hopeful there are other things I can do for LNO. Money isn't everything."

"Exactly. And I'm sure Annie is thankful for the time you give to her organization."

"So, what made you want to be a journalist?"

"Simply put, and to spare you from hours of boredom, I believe in finding out the facts of a situation, reporting what I believe to be the truth, thus allowing the reader to make up his or her own mind on an issue."

She nodded, never taking her eyes off him. "What do you think of a reporter who manipulates the facts to fit his story, or who puts their own spin on it?"

"Truthfully, I don't have much respect for that person. It's not easy to find a reporter who shares all sides of an issue and those who don't, belong in the opinion section of the paper. A good reporter is worth a lot in my estimation."

"So you consider yourself a harbinger of the truth. How noble of you."

It was difficult to dismiss her scathing tone. Her barb had certainly hit home. She just didn't know it.

"I'm sorry," she said. "There goes that broad brush again."

She ran her finger around the rim of her mug. "However, what if you think you have the facts, but they turn out to be wrong and you don't realize they're wrong, and you end up reporting a story that's false, thereby hurting the party or parties in question?" She glanced up—blatant, unabashed, antagonism spilling from her honey-brown eyes. "Not just hurting their company, but their reputation?"

He tapped his finger on the arm of the chair. That was a loaded question if he ever heard one. There was absolutely no way she could know his identity. "I would retract the information in the article."

"After the damage had been done?" She leaned forward and spoke softly, but clear enough that he heard her. "Sounds like a simple fix on your end, but what about the person or even an entire organization who's been maligned?"

His article had done more than hurt, she'd been devastated by it.

"He or she would undoubtedly have a tough time of things, but hopefully only for a while."

She sat back aghast. "That's it? No apology? That would make it all right with you as the author?"

"Of course not."

"How would you find out that the mistake had been made?"

He couldn't help but be moved by the earnest plea in her voice. But, he hadn't made a mistake.

"I wouldn't unless someone or some other event brought it to my attention."

"I see." She swallowed hard and stood. "Do you have any other questions? I really should get back to work."

"Nope." Cam stood and slipped his arms into his coat. "I think I have everything I need for now."

As Jill walked him to the entrance, he said, "Look, could we call a halt to this antagonist behavior?" He had a lot of nerve asking her that, but she didn't know it. And what she didn't know, well... If he was going to get anywhere with this article they needed to be more than civil.

She folded her arms. "I've had a bad experience with a journalist." She glanced down at her shoes, then back up at him. "I know better than to assume you're all alike. But this whole thing is recent and I'm still upset about it."

"What did the article say exactly?" He held his breath.

"It's kind of hard to explain. I mean he didn't even mention my name. I guess I should be thankful for that." She gave a weak unconvincing chuckle. "It's just...if someone in my industry figures out it's me, they could interpret it...very badly." She threw her hands in the air. "Anyway, it's nothing to do with you. So please accept my apology."

"No need. I get it."

"Okay. Good." Something close to relief flowed from her eyes. "And stop by anytime you have any questions. Otherwise, I'll see you Saturday."

Cam approached the elevator and pressed the call button. He hadn't felt like a jerk since high school. He scrubbed his hand across his mouth. What he'd written were the facts. He'd done his job. The truth hurts and it had hurt her. The article was out there. Nothing he could do about it now.

As far as he could tell, the piece had only hurt her pride and not her business. His hope was that it would bring attention to the plight of the homeless and nothing more. In that moment he came to a decision. He'd come up with some excuse to continue seeing her beyond the two-week commitment. That way, if she lost work he'd at least know about it.

CHAPTER TWELVE

Jill measured off two and a half yards from the ream of fabric next to the pattern she'd created for the Saturday morning high school session. She'd chosen a periwinkle blue, a color that would look great on any skin tone. The dress was a simple A-line. An easy classic design for beginners.

She positioned the left front of the pattern, then the right and pinned them in place. As she slid the scissors between the table and the fabric someone knocked on the door.

She glanced at the workroom clock. Everyone had already gone home well over an hour ago. She stood, feet planted and listened. She wasn't expecting anyone and it was unusual for someone to just show up. Especially, after hours.

There it was again. Louder this time. She kept the scissors in her hand and approached the door. "Who is it?"

"Cameron."

"Oh." She cracked the door open. He stood there holding up a white grocery sack and a six-pack of bottled water. He eyed the scissors. "I hope I didn't frighten you."

"No, I always answer the door with scissors."

"May I come in?"

"Please." She stepped back, heart thudding at his sudden appearance. Could the man get any more handsome? "What's up?"

"I was in the neighborhood."

"Sure you were."

He grinned. "I have more questions and it's been a long day. I was hungry and took a chance you were here and also hungry."

"I think you have spies." She chuckled. "So happens I am hungry." She gave a half nod at the bag in his hand. "You can put that down over here."

He followed her to one of the smaller tables in the workroom. "Do you usually work this late?"

"Sometimes. We've had a few new clients lately. Coupled with my regulars means longer hours for me."

He glanced at her worktable. "Did I catch you in the middle of something?"

"It can wait." She placed the offending scissors on the work-table. She found it difficult not to watch him as he lifted out the food boxes with well-groomed and very capable looking hands.

She bit her thumbnail and studied him. He was casually dressed in dark pants and a navy sweater, which showcased his lean physique. This was the first time she'd had the opportunity to really look at him and the sudden intimacy of his close prox-imity made her heart flutter. Her gaze traveled to his face, which held strength and purpose and a set of eyelashes most girls would kill for. Cameron Phillips certainly had the wow factor. She won-dered if he'd ever considered modeling.

"Earth to Jill."

"What?" She blinked twice and lowered her thumb.

A flicker of a smile tugged the corners of his mouth. Great. He'd caught her staring. She cleared her throat. "What's for dinner?"

"I wasn't sure what you liked so I brought several options. Sweet and sour pork, Kung Pao chicken, wonton soup, fried rice, and spring rolls.

"Ooo, I'll take the chicken and a spring roll."

Once they settled down to eat, Jill with chopsticks in mid-air, asked. "So. Why are you really here?"

Cam shot her a quick glance, then as if wanting to delay his response he untwisted the water bottle cap and took a generous swig. "Okay, I admit it. I do have an ulterior motive."

Curious as to what that could be, she waited.

"There's a group of teenage girls that are homeless. They live in an all-girls boarding school for orphans just outside the city. I was wondering if you'd do a session with them. It wouldn't have to be the four Saturdays a month, but something shorter. Maybe a one-time thing? We could ride out together if you'd like."

She gazed at him like she was seeing him for the first time. Forever on high alert whenever he was around, this was the last request she would have expected from him.

"Did I suddenly grow another head?" The corners of his mouth lifted.

"I'm a little surprised, that's all. You...getting into all of this. Of course I'll have a session with them. Do you have a particular time or day in mind?"

"I wanted to ask you first. I haven't even approached the lady in charge yet."

"Okay. You talk with her and I'll look at my calendar and see what I can work out. How does that sound?"

"Sounds great."

After they finished their meal, Jill went to wash up. When she came back, Cam was perusing her pattern on the worktable.

"Is this how you start all your designs?"

"Initially, I start on paper. Brainstorming ideas until I come up with something I like. Then I do a detailed sketch that I eventually transfer to pattern paper. After that I cut out the pattern, then pin it onto a dressmaker's form. Once I see that it fits, I transfer the design to fabric and pin that onto the form. When that's done, I study it and add notions, like a belt, or buttons or a collar or sleeves."

"Interesting."

"Of course, every designer has their own method, their own particular way of doing things."

"You do this all by yourself?"

"Pretty much, although I do have help now with the actual pattern making and sewing. It gives me time for creating more designs."

"So what's this one for?"

"It's the surprise for my Saturday morning session at the high school."

"Oh, right."

She handed him a pair of scissors. "Would you like to help? It'll go faster with two of us."

"I'm all yours."

For a moment, her gaze held his and even though she knew the context in which he'd said those three little words, she found herself wondering what it would be like to be all his. She released a breath and cleared her throat.

"Cut this one out, then, and I'll take care of the back sections at the other end of the table."

They worked quietly side by side. Twenty minutes later Jill had the pieces pinned together and hanging on the dressmaker's form.

"Now for the fun part." Jill stepped over to the container wall. After carefully perusing the shelves, she returned with two square bins. "Let's look through these and see if something grabs our eye."

They played around with several ideas, but nothing satisfied Jill.

Cam chose a large yellow button. "I like this." He held it against the center of the dress.

"Go higher," Jill said. "Stop, right there." Jill held the button in place with a pin. "Because the dress is simple, I think three buttons might look nice. Angled, like so." She picked up two more of the yellow and pinned them at an angle toward the shoulder. "What do you think?"

"This looks great. I can't believe the difference such a simple solution made to the appearance." He smiled down at her. "You got any coffee?"

"Addicting, isn't it?"

"The coffee or the dress making?"

"Both I guess." She smiled.

"I can see why you enjoy your job."

Minutes later, they sat on the sofa in the entrance area and sipped on the hot liquid.

"Your Christmas tree is amazing. I've never seen spools of thread or buttons used as garland. I especially like the small multi-colored scissors throughout the branches."

"Thanks. Except for the twinkle lights, there's not one traditional ornament on the tree. We had a blast decorating it."

He nodded. "So. How did you get started in this business?" he asked.

"I've always loved designing clothes. When I was a kid I'd make clothes for my dolls and for the cat."

"Poor cat."

"I know." She lifted the mug to her mouth and sipped. "I've loved color and basically anything fun. And I've never liked the matchy-matchy look. But, somehow all my mix and match of fabrics and textures seemed to work. I went to art school in Maryland, then got my first job with a clothing designer, where I continued to learn the business and the art. Eventually, I'd made enough to try it on my own."

"Left the comforts of the Jeffrey nest and spread your wings."

"Um." She chuckled. "Yeah, something like that."

This man perplexed her. Like Mark, he'd undoubtedly assumed she was a Scarsdale Jeffrey and that suited her just fine.

She was beginning to like Cameron Phillips, but knew she meant absolutely nothing to him. Heck, they barely knew each another. She'd been dropped by one of the wealthiest men in New York. A man who only cared about social position. It was easy to assume Cameron Phillips ran in Mark's circles. She had little hope of impressing Cam as a Jeffrey of Paige Point. Better for him to believe she was someone else.

* * *

The sewing session the following Saturday was a huge success. Each girl left with a simple, but classic custom-made design. Cam didn't make an appearance, which surprised her after his most recent avid interest in the subject. He was definitely one of the most perplexing and aggravating men she'd ever met. Maybe he'd realized he had all the info he needed for his article, making her wonder if he'd even show up for the afternoon session. She hoped that wasn't the case. Aggravating or not, she rather liked the way he'd simply showed up unannounced.

At noon, Jill grabbed a meatloaf panini at Press 195, then headed to Billings Community Center in Queens. She'd just placed the last LNO gift package at each chair when her group of fourteen and fifteen-year-old girls entered the room.

In the middle of her opening remarks, Cameron slipped through the side door, shrugged out of his jacket and quietly took a seat along the back wall.

He was dressed in jeans and a dark, long-sleeved V-neck t-shirt. Nothing fancy or anything that said, *designer*, but it definitely looked fantastic on him. He flipped open his narrow notepad, then placed it on one knee.

She raised her gaze to his and caught him staring at her. By the expression on his face it was obvious he'd been watching her the entire time she'd surveyed his physique and clothing. Flustered, she glanced away. She needed to be more careful with her moments of perusal. For some reason, being under his scrutiny still unnerved her. As a journalist he probably picked up on more than he let on. Heaven forbid he should misinterpret some word or phrase while she led the workshop. It could undermine everything LNO had been trying to undo since the Alex Langdon scandal.

The Eagle Eye article had heightened her damage control antenna to the extreme. So far she'd been lucky nothing too terrible had happened. But hanging with a journalist for two weeks was quite a different story. One amiable meal over Asian cuisine did not make him any less the reporter. In her limited experience, reporters were interested in one thing—a Pulitzer—and it mattered little to them who they hurt to get it.

As the girls opened up their colorful, Like No Other notebooks, she shot him another glance. There was a smile in his eyes as if he held a secret, something only he knew. Unable to break the connection, she was helpless to do anything but stare back at him. With one look he pulled her in and kept her riveted. Held her spellbound. She blinked nervously and refocused on the group of girls in front of her.

"When I was fourteen, all of my friends had grown a lot taller than me," Jill said. "Because I'd always wanted to be in fashion, I was pretty bummed about my height. You see, I wanted to be an international high-fashion model. But, I had two things against me. My height *and* my weight."

An audible gasp filled the room.

"That's right. I didn't always look like I do now." She twirled in place and struck a pose. "I know what it's like to struggle with weight. I wasn't as thin as many of my classmates, especially the tall girls. It's one of the reasons I started making my own clothes. I learned how to cover certain areas and enhance others. So like many teenagers, I developed some self-image issues. Which is perfectly normal, by the way. You are not alone."

"I hate my nose," a short girl on the front row said through her giggles.

The room peppered with laughter.

"And I hate my freckles," added another.

"You see." Jill laughed. She hopped up on the presentation table, crossed her legs at her ankles and swung them back and forth.

"When I was growing up, my mother called me her little snowflake. I used to love that. But, it wasn't until I started moaning about my height and weight that I fully understood what she had been trying to instill in me."

She slid off the table and stood before them. "It's like this. Think of all the snow that has fallen…let's say…on the Rocky Mountains. All that snow came down from the sky, one snowflake at a time. And here's the amazing part, something I know you all learned in first grade. But I'm going to repeat it, anyway. Not one of those flakes is like another. Each is one of a kind. Unique, special, tiny, yet perfect.

"You…are so much more amazing then any snowflake. No one has *ever* looked like you. Think about that. Your DNA makes you one of a kind…beautifully and wonderfully made. And… yes, I am getting carried away again."

Laughter broke out across the room.

"Okay, everybody, that's it for today. Remember, I'm just an email away."

Jill tugged her thick lime green sweater around her torso, then followed the girls outside. After she saw the last girl safely into her mother's car she turned toward Cam, who stood watching just a few yards away.

"You know." She approached him. "It's all right if you speak to them. They don't bite."

"There's plenty of time for that," Cam said. "Right now, I'm gathering info by observing the interaction between all of you. It's amazing how much I'm gathering simply by watching and listening."

He stood gazing at the car driving away and something about the way he looked at it reminded her of—*Oh, my gosh. Phil.* She sucked in an audible breath.

He turned toward her. "What is it? What's wrong?"

"You just…" She shook her head. "It's nothing."

"Are you sure?"

"I'm sure."

What was wrong with her? Obviously, she was seeing things. That's what happened from weeks of obsessive searching.

"I see you're wearing the dress we made the other night."

"I am." Glancing down, she tugged apart the front of the bulky sweater. "Cute, huh?"

"It is… Would you, um…like to go to a party with me?"

She blinked. "Are you asking me out? On a date?"

Cam placed a finger under her chin. An amused twinkle filled his eyes. "Is that so surprising?"

"Yes. I mean… Our relationship has been anything, but platonic."

"Maybe on your side. But you don't speak for me."

"Oh."

Cam took her hand and led her to a bench in front of the community center. "Sit down."

Jill sat, never taking her gaze off his face.

"Monday evening the associated press is having a cocktail party for a select group of journalists in the area. Would you like to go?"

She continued to gaze at him, wondering what his motives could be. She shook her internal head. When did she become so suspicious of people?

"My editor wants me there and since I'm on deadline with another article I could use that time to continue our interview. What do you say?"

"So, it's more of a business thing."

"That's one way to look at it."

"Sure." She lifted a shoulder. "If it helps you out, that's fine. I'm happy to go."

"Great, I'll pick you up at seven."

Chapter Thirteen

Jill placed the bag of popcorn in the microwave, then stood aside contemplating the Cameron issue. She guessed she liked him. She found him extremely attractive. Nothing not to like about that. But, she wasn't about to put much stock in the fact that he'd asked her out. After all, it was only a business thing. But the fact that he'd planned to pick her up and not have her meet him, was a plus.

In their short time together, he'd yet to show any real interest in her, and other than a few personal questions during his interview sessions, most of their conversation was limited to all things *Annie* and *Like No Other*.

If he were interested in her, he had an odd way of showing it. Rather secretive, as if he were pacing himself. Could he be uncertain of her response? Impossible. The man oozed confidence.

Three minutes later, she pulled the hot snack from her microwave and dumped it carefully in her vintage 1940's green mixing bowl. She settled onto the living room sofa and dove her hand into the buttery dish. She'd found the bowl one Sunday after she'd moved to New York at a garage sale in Queens. She'd arrived in the city, mostly broke, and thanks to family hand-me-downs and local area weekend garage sales, she'd managed to supply her tiny apartment with a few necessities.

That was three years ago. Two and a half years later she'd moved into the brownstone, having sold her garage sale finds to the woman now renting the apartment.

'Don't forget where you came from, Jill.' Her dad had told her on the day she'd left home. He then slipped three hundred dollars cash into her right hand with a swift kiss on her left cheek.

Now, curled up on Daniel Livingston's living room sofa, she opened Safari on her laptop and crammed a handful of popcorn between her lips.

Her search on The Eagle Eye had produced zero results. Everything she'd pulled up focused on the articles with very little speculation as to the author's real identity. She knew the writer was a man because of how he referred to himself throughout each piece.

After a further search, she found two articles from earlier months and clicked on the one about underage drinking. Deep, heartfelt, and totally relatable, he wrote as if from personal experience. It was good and Jill had to admit she agreed with everything he'd said. He stood out from the rest—the raw, no-holds-barred touch of venom, his trademark. She could see why his audience loved him. Admittedly, the venom seemed appropriate in this particular piece, but totally inaccurate when pointed at her.

Even with all of that, he somehow managed to leave his readers with hope. But his targeted remarks in the homeless article seemed more personal, as if she'd offended him in some way.

She took a swig of root beer and continued her search. She found two more, both published by the *New York Post*.

"He had to be a New Yorker." She leaned her head against the back of the sofa and heaved a frustrated sigh. Oh sure, easy. There were only hundreds of newspaper journalists in this city. And finding the right one should be *no* problem.

She typed Cameron's name in the search bar. A whole string of articles came up. She clicked on one about mothers gardening with their children. It turned out to be a heartwarming, light-hearted piece. She opened up two more and scanned them. Both similar to the first one, peaking her interest in each topic covered. Reading these gave her an added glimpse into the man. Now there was a nice guy, nothing like that bottom dweller.

She closed her laptop with the hope she would find some answers at the Associated Press gathering Cam had invited her to.

* * *

Cameron stood at Jill's brownstone on East Fifty-Seventh Street and knocked. Ten years working in New York, and he'd never made enough to buy a brownstone, much less in this high-end part of the city. As a Scarsdale Jeffrey, he shouldn't be surprised.

A few seconds later, the door opened. Jill stood before him, a vision in pink. She wore a simple, but elegant dress, the deep rosy hues bringing out her caramel eyes. She'd swept her hair up, securing it with a long, sparkly clip. That coupled with her spiked heels added at least three inches to her height. A short strand of pearls lay across her delicate collarbone, accentuating her creamy complexion.

She was gorgeous.

Jill peered up at him and scrunched her nose. "Too much?"

"Not at all. You look fabulous."

She let out a breath as if his opinion had mattered to her. "Please, come in while I get my coat."

He stepped inside and waited while she disappeared down the hall. He stood in the center of the wide foyer and perused the art on her walls. Expensive tastes for one so young. Probably influenced by her family. He knew personally the rewards of growing up with money.

His gaze fell on a rectangular framed photo perched on the edge of the antique bow-front chest. He picked it up and studied it. Jill was pictured with six other adults in what looked like a kitchen cafeteria.

Minutes later she was back carrying a black wool overcoat. At her approach, he set the photo down. "May I?" He took the coat and held it while she turned her back to him. As she slid her arms through the sleeves, his gaze roamed along her bare shoulders to the nape of her neck where a soft tendril had escaped its clasp. Without thinking, he lifted the stray lock and tucked it back in place.

"Thank you." Jill fingered where he'd tucked the wayward strand and smiled.

"Nice digs."

"Thanks." A pink glow covered her cheeks. "Shall we go?"

Cameron drove them to The Peninsula and handed his keys to the valet while a second attendant opened the passenger door for Jill. As Cam rounded the front of the car he noticed Jill walking toward the corner. He'd made his way to her side just as she approached a shabbily dressed man holding a sign. Cam gnawed the inside of his lip and waited.

Jill took a tentative step closer to the man, who hadn't yet noticed her approach. She glanced at his face and spoke. Her kind smile as she gazed at the guy tugged against his ribs. She then took something from her purse and handed it to him. Head lowered, she slowly walked back to Cam.

"Are you all right?"

"Yes."

"What was that about?" He nodded toward the street person.

"Nothing." She gave a half smile. "Let's go in?"

As she stepped forward, he gently placed his hand on her wrist, stopping her. "You seem disappointed."

She glanced over her shoulder, back at the man on the corner. "A case of mistaken identity."

"You're looking for a street person?"

A resigned expression crossed her face. "And I suppose you think I'm crazy, too?"

"Who else thinks that?"

"A couple of people. No one you'd know."

"Ever think that maybe they're right?"

"Sure. I mean, I go to places most women wouldn't dream of going. But if you could see some of the conditions Annie's girls live in. You'd go, too."

He knew about her visit to the abandoned subway, but couldn't help wonder what other risky behavior she was into. "Are you actually visiting dangerous places in the city?"

"Not dangerous really, but definitely questionable as to how safe they are."

"What's the difference?"

"Do we have to talk about this now? Here?"

"No. We don't." For a moment all he could do was stare at her. "Let's go in."

Ten minutes later, they entered a small contemporary ballroom on the fourth floor, where Dick Powel and his wife immediately greeted Cam.

"Jill, this is Dick Powel, my editor and his wife, Ellen."

The three shook hands.

"So, Jill, what do you do?" Ellen asked.

"I'm a fashion designer here in New York."

"Anything I'd be familiar with?"

"Not unless you have a teenage daughter."

"Not one of my own, but I've worked with several teenage girls in the city."

"Ellen is with child services," Cam said.

"By the way, Cam," Ellen said, "I wanted to let you know your protégé has been taken care of."

"Protégé?" Jill asked.

"Your boyfriend here—"

"Oh, we're not…" Jill spoke quickly.

"I just happened to be at the right place at the right time." Cam nipped any further conversation with Ellen with a pointed look and a quick shake of his head.

He then turned to Jill. "Let's mingle."

He pulled Jill's arm through his own and led her across the room. "Sorry about that. Ellen can be a bit…"

"Don't worry, it's fine." Jill laughed. "Really. They seem to be very nice people."

"They are."

"So, Dick's your editor."

"Yes, although I've recently gone freelance."

"That seems rash."

"I'll still write a weekly article for him at the *Post*, but will have more free time to follow my own instincts as far as stories go. Freelance will enable me to do both."

"You must do well to give up a regular paying job."

"I get by." He nodded. "And I'm fortunate. Not everyone gets to do what they love."

"Tell me about your work as a journalist," she said.

"It usually starts with an assignment from an editor, but sometimes I have an idea or a particular story I'd like to cover and I can do that more now that I'm freelance. Then there's the research, interviews—"

"And shadowing a person, like what you're doing with me."

"Yes, that too."

"How many years have you been in the business?"

"Ten."

"Nice. So. You must know a lot of people in the industry."

Her sudden interest and penetrating gaze sounded a warning bell in his head. "I know a fair amount."

"Editors, photographers, journalists…"

He nodded, eyeing her. "Why do I get the feeling you're interviewing me?"

"Um." Her gaze dropped to somewhere around the top button on his shirt. She tucked a wayward strand of hair behind her ear. "I'm just curious, that's all."

She glanced around the room. His gaze followed her direction.

"Maybe if you'd just tell me who it is you're looking for I could help?"

She turned her attention back to him, wide-eyed, and open-mouthed. "I'm not looking for anyone. I'm…admiring the fashion. Very exclusive and high-end garments. Quite nice."

Sure, it's the fashion.

At that moment, one of his colleagues, Mick Samuel, approached them.

"Jill, Mick. Mick, Jill Jeffrey."

Jill brightened. "Hi, Mick. What type of stories do you write?"

For the next hour, Cam introduced Jill to as many in his industry as time would allow. With each intro, Jill turned on the charm - her focused, pointed questions obvious only to him. His colleagues never suspected her query was anything more than an avid interest in them and their work. But he knew differently. Knew why she asked the questions—knew who it was she looked for. And also knew she'd never find him. At least not the way she was going about it.

Admittedly, the back and forth between her and each reporter she met amused him. As the evening progressed, resulting in little or no information as to the Eagle's identity, he couldn't help but be touched by her obvious disappointment. He realized for Jill, this was no laughing matter.

But after enduring fifteen minutes of Jason Klein's blow-by-blow account of his latest article, he felt the need to intervene.

"Jason, may I have a word with Jill?"

"Absolutely." Jason shook Jill's hand and left.

"I thought he'd never stop." Jill gushed her relief. "Thank you."

"My pleasure. Would you like a drink?"

"I'd love one."

"Anything in particular?"

"Whatever you're having is fine." She fluttered her hand in the air in a dismissive gesture.

* * *

Jill scanned the room, focusing on the male journalists at the party. What a total, complete waste of time. Not only had her research produced absolutely nothing, but so had the interviews. She may as well face it. This whole endeavor to find the Eagle was hopeless. She had absolutely nothing to go on and never would.

While Jill waited for Cam to return with the drinks, an elderly lady approached her, followed by a second woman.

"Oh, my dear, I couldn't help but overhear when your young man introduced you. Are you one of the Jeffreys of Scarsdale?"

The thought crossed Jill's mind that it was highly possible she'd entered a parallel universe. She blinked and focused on the sweet-looking lady in front of her.

"My daughter, Margo Simmons, had dinner at your estate last month for a fundraiser, and she's talked of nothing else since. Were you present and do you recall meeting her by any chance? She's petite like you, but with strawberry blonde hair."

Jill sighed inwardly. Even sweet old ladies assumed she was part of that family.

"Millicent," the second lady said, "don't bother this young woman."

Millicent stepped closer to Jill. "I'm sorry, but my sister gets a little confused sometimes."

"I heard that, Millicent. I'm not confused. Margo told me so herself."

Oh dear.

Jill gazed at the eager and openly distressed older woman and didn't have the heart to disappoint her. "No, ma'am. I wasn't there." Jill glanced from one sister to the other. "Thank you so much for your kind words, though. The estate is quite something and I'm so happy your daughter had such a lovely time at the event."

Cam had returned and stood listening while holding the drinks.

"I understand your home has been in and out of the Jeffrey family for generations," the lady said.

"Yeeesss, it has."

"You must be thrilled to have it back again now."

"That…is also true," Jill said.

"Well. I see your young man has returned. It was a pleasure meeting you. Enjoy the rest of your evening."

The ladies walked away and Jill watched, opened mouthed.

"I couldn't help but overhear. A friend of the family?"

"Seems like." Jill accepted the glass of Chardonnay from Cam and continued to eye them as they crossed the room. "Such sweet ladies."

Hopefully, he hadn't overheard too much of the conversation, but it didn't really matter since he'd already assumed she was a Scarsdale Jeffrey. Not that anything was wrong with that rich and famous family. She didn't even know them.

"So it's now confirmed. You are a Jeffrey of Scarsdale. I thought as much."

She whipped around ready to deny it, but the mocking gleam in his eye stopped her. "Why Mr. Phillips, I had no idea you were such a snob." She raised her chin and her brow for effect.

"You think I'm a snob?"

"Well, what else am I supposed to surmise after that comment?"

"I see nothing wrong with what I said."

"It was more your tone, than your actual words." She wondered if she should just tell him now that she wasn't one of those Jeffreys. But, he'd acted somewhat of a pill toward her since the day they'd met. Let him think what he wanted.

"Tell me, is it just my family or all of Scarsdale you dislike?"

"When have I ever given you the impression I don't like you?"

"Since the moment we met in Annie's office. Remember?"

"To my recollection we've already established that was a misunderstanding on my part."

"Then it must be Scarsdale, then. Seriously, you don't find Scarsdale's old English architecture, Tudor estate homes and the lack of large box stores charming?"

"Utterly charming." He shrugged. "It's some of the people I have issue with."

"Oh." She lifted the wine to her lips, and grimaced at the taste, wondering who he despised in Scarsdale. An old girlfriend, maybe? "I thought someone who wrote for the *Post* would feel quite comfortable there. All those doctors and lawyers and such."

"I have nothing against wealthy, professional people. My grandfather is from there and was quite a successful lawyer in his day."

She twirled the wine glass and eyed him critically.

* * *

Cam found her direct stare unnerving. Even with his near foolproof disguise, Cam knew it was only a matter of time before she figured out who he was. Maybe his plan to spend more time with her wasn't his best idea.

"Have we met, before?" she blurted out.

He locked his gaze with hers. "What makes you say that?"

"I don't know. Something about the way you just tilted your head and…and your eyes, they…" She held his gaze for a moment longer, then shook her head as if clearing cobwebs. "Forget it."

He let out a breath. For a second, he'd thought the jig was up. He'd been concerned she'd recognize him since Annie suggested he and Jill work together. But, at the moment Jill's abrupt change and thoughtful frown made him want to know what was going on in that head of hers.

"Something wrong?" he asked.

She raised her gaze to his. "No." She shrugged. "I was just thinking of someone. The person you reminded me of."

"Do I still remind you of him? It is a *him*?"

A tiny laugh escaped her lips. "It is indeed." She threw down the last bit of wine, scrunched up her nose and shivered.

"Let me guess, an old boyfriend? Someone you dropped flat and are now feeling sorry about it?"

"No."

"Someone who dumped you, then?" he said in a teasing manner.

"No, no." She shook her head. "Nothing like that. Although, I have been dumped." She ran a finger around the rim of her empty glass.

Jill continued to amaze him. What beautiful young woman admits to being dumped? Especially to a reporter writing a story that included her.

"Come on." He leaned forward at the waist and whispered. "Tell Uncle Cam about it."

She giggled.

Good, she'd loosened up. Alcohol did have its virtues, even to one who obviously found it distasteful. As he eyed her, she paused and gazed ahead as if deep in thought.

Her lips formed the sweetest smile, but her eyes held a hint of regret that touched him.

Then she added in a rush, "You're a reporter."

"I am."

"How do you go about finding someone?"

"Facebook?"

"No, that wouldn't work in this case. I hardly know him."

"And is this the *him* that brought the wistful expression to your face?"

"It's not what you think."

"And what is it I'm supposed to think?"

"It's just someone I met and I'd like to find him, that's all. I just want to make sure he's all right." She signaled to a waiter about to pass by and placed her glass on his tray. "I'm concerned that he might have gotten hurt or something."

"A missing person. Now that is interesting."

She let out a frustrated breath and nodded.

"Then, I'd probably start with the police. Give them a description, his name, the last time you saw him, details like that."

"Okaaay." An engaging frown knit her features.

"Now what's the problem?" he asked.

"I don't actually know his name. At least not his full one."

"Then start with what you do know and let the police take it from there."

* * *

Cameron walked Jill up the steps to her brownstone, surprised at how much he'd enjoyed the evening. When they reached the door, she pulled the key from her beaded purse and turned to him. "Thank you for inviting me to the party. I had a lovely time."

"I'm glad." For a brief second they stood staring at each other. "Who dumped you?"

Jill's eyes widened. "That's not the question I was anticipating."

"I know. But, it's bugged me all evening. Is the guy nuts?"

She smiled sweetly. "What a nice thing to say." Her gaze fluttered to the knot in his tie before returning to his face. "He's not nuts, just highly particular."

"You know I never did get to ask you my follow-up questions. Could we get together tomorrow sometime? Or if it's not too late, I could come in."

Jill's eyes grew enormous.

"Or not."

"Monday would be better for me. I'm actually quite tired."

"I understand."

"No, really I am."

He loved how she tried so hard to make him believe it.

"I was up until four this morning making this dress."

"You made this?"

"Yes. You've seen my wardrobe. Teenageville. I had nothing appropriate for tonight so I made something. It's what I do. And I had to be at the office at nine this morning for a business meeting. So…"

"I hear you."

"Come by the office anytime on Monday." One second later she stepped inside her brownstone and had shut the massive door in his face.

"Okaaay." Cam shoved his hands into his coat pockets. "Monday it is."

Chapter Fourteen

It was almost lunch time when Jill pushed through the door of the New Hope Soup Kitchen. Pot roast Sunday. She could smell the mouth-watering dish as soon as she entered the building.

"Jill!" The owner, Spencer Keith, waved her to the back of the cafeteria counter.

"Hey, Spencer."

Spencer's massive form enveloped her in the hug of all hugs. "Take over, Bret. This young lady and I have business to discuss." Spencer untied his apron and motioned to Jill.

She followed him to the back office and took a chair. "It's good to see you."

Warmth filled his eyes. "And you."

"You have a nice group today."

"It's grown some since you left us." His gaze held a note of concern. "But tell me, how are you?"

"Well, my design business is starting to take off. Finally."

"Good. Good. But that's not—"

"I didn't see any of the regulars out there."

Smiling slightly, he glanced at the floor. "Oh, they'll be along soon. So. What brings you back here today?"

"There's this guy, Phil. He lives on the street. I was wondering if you could help find him a job. That is, if I can find him, again."

"What does he do?"

"He's a writer."

"Oh, that's a tough one."

"I know."

"Look, Jill. I'm happy to meet him, but finding him work is another matter. Do you need help locating him? I could send Bret with you. He has a nose for these things."

"That won't be necessary. Unless he's moved on, I think I know where he is."

He nodded. "Bring him by next week. I may have something for him then. If not, I can at least give him a hot meal and a place to sleep."

She stood. "Great."

They made their way back to the front entrance.

"Would you like to serve the green beans? It'll be like old times."

Jill glanced at the men and women forming the line. Some of them stood shoulder slumped, eyes mirroring hopelessness. "I don't think so. I...I have to get back to work."

Spencer gripped her hand. "It wasn't your fault, you know. Some people just don't want to be helped."

"I know."

* * *

Sunday afternoon, Cameron stood in front of his bathroom mirror and applied a thin layer of spirit gum to the lower half of his face, waited twenty seconds, then carefully attached the fake beard - compliments of a buddy of his who worked in the theatre district. For a moment he studied his reflection. Phil looked nothing like Cameron. It was just too weird.

He tapped his fingers above his upper lip, then pulled a New York Mets baseball cap over his head. The cap had about two inches of hair extensions added to the edges. He'd used the beard and hair-hat during the first two weeks of his undercover research, until his own hair and beard had grown out.

He'd chosen to spend the afternoon on the streets and in the tent city. In a strange way he'd missed it. Missed the people-watching and the late-night conversations with Eddie. Emotionally, he'd been pulled in many directions during his month under-cover. He would never be the same.

He slapped his hands several times against his arms and shivered. Even though the sun was shining you wouldn't know it standing on the street. The vertical city of New York blocked out most, if not all, the sun's rays and one had to find just the right spot to get any warmth.

After several slow, perusing trips through the tent city, he finally decided to call it quits. Two subway stops later, he got off the train and mounted the steps to Fifth Avenue.

He walked half a block and noticed his corner was vacant near the iconic luxury hotel and the park. He thought of Jill and wondered if she still searched for him. It wasn't like 'Cam' could just come out and ask her. Gnawing his lower lip, he came to a decision. After all, he was certainly dressed for the part. He crossed the street, lowered his backpack to his feet, then held up his sign and waited.

He took the moment to study The Plaza. One of the most photographed and iconic places in New York and he never tired of it. Christmas lights were everywhere and especially beautiful in this part of town. The hustle and bustle of shoppers streamed in and out of some of the finest stores in the city. Fifth Avenue and Central Park South. Nothing like it.

"Phil?"

He froze. Oh, no. It couldn't be. He inched around to face a pair of glowing eyes. Lord help him. Holding an enormous Bergdorf Goodman shopping bag in each hand, Jill stood before him, wrapped in a bundle of green cashmere, wearing snug jeans and black boots. The top of her head sported a matching beret, and she wore a sparkling smile he couldn't help but respond to.

"As I live and breathe. Miss Jillian Jeffrey."

"I thought I'd lost you."

He placed one hand over his heart. "I'm right here."

He needed to take note of the sound of his voice. Now that he'd spent time with her as Cam, it was highly probable she'd be able to recognize it. He cleared his throat and faked a cough.

"I know, but I looked for you for weeks after that afternoon in the tent city." Lifting her finger, she made a circle motion around her face. "Your beard. It's gotten longer."

He nodded. Best not to speak unless he had to.

She was totally and completely animated. Not even his own mother was ever this excited to see him. He couldn't help but smile. She was the most engaging creature he'd ever met. In that moment he could honestly say, he was pleased to know her under his real name and occupation. Someday Phil would simply fade away. He hoped it wouldn't break her heart, too much. She was wreathed in smiles and gazing up at him like he was some sort of a god.

He lowered his voice a bit. "You're certainly into the swing of the holiday season," he said.

She lifted the large bags still in each hand. "I know."

He leaned forward at the waist and peeked inside. "Looks like your family and friends will have quite a Christmas."

"Yes, well, I tend to overdo it a bit. But right now, I'm taking you to dinner. Here, hold this." She gave him one of the festive sacks, grabbed his free hand, then pulled him alongside her. "There's a sandwich shop across the street near the park."

He allowed her to lead him through the wide square, and past the giant shrub encased in a million twinkle lights. The fact that he knew her made the difference, but what intrigued him most was that she would do this for him. A stranger. A street bum.

They entered the restaurant and shrugged out of their coats and gloves. Two minutes later, they were seated at the window overlooking the busy thoroughfare. After they ordered the soup special and a sandwich, Jill lifted a box from one of the shopping bags.

"I want to give you something." She pulled out a men's cherry-red neck scarf, then looped it around his neck. "It's alpaca wool and just your color."

Immensely touched, he fingered the soft material. "This is very nice, but I'm sure you bought it for someone else." He started to remove it.

"No, please. I want you to have it. It'll mean so much to me if you'd accept it."

He gazed into her sincere face. A million things ran through his head. Who was this young woman? Where did she come from? One moment a rare minx, the next, sweet and thoughtful and so willing to help others.

Why was she so taken with Phil? With Phil, she was happy, animated, unreserved. A lot like she was when teaching the teenage girls. But with Cam, she was far more measured and thoughtful. As if she feared she'd slip and say something she'd later regret.

After his article, she had every right to fear the big, bad reporter. The Eagle had hurt her. *Cameron* had hurt her. But not Phil. Jill had a heart for helping others and she'd made it clear she'd wanted to help him. Not once had she demonstrated fear in his presence. In the past, he'd thought her either foolish or stupid. Now he realized she was neither and he felt badly deceiving her.

"All right. I accept. Thank you."

The waitress set the hot plates in front of them. "Can I get you anything else?"

"No thanks," Jill said.

"I'm good."

Jill tipped her spoon into the savory stew and blew across the top. "May I ask you a question?"

"Of course."

"The night we met and I invited you in for dinner. Did someone approach you, like a reporter?"

"No."

She eyed him from across the table. "So you weren't interviewed by a newspaper man?"

"No." He faked a cough and cleared his throat. "No one asked me anything."

"Okay."

"Why?"

"It's nothing really." She lifted a shoulder. "I was just wondering."

Actually, it was more like a *big* something. He knew the Eagle's influence. In his weaker moments he'd experienced a stab of regret over the article. Even with all the accolades after it had come out, he'd still felt he might have overreached in the way he'd referred to her. As far as he knew, her peers hadn't identified her as the teen designer from the article. But the fact that she was asking made him wonder.

"May I ask *you* a question?" he said.

"Sure."

"Why did you continue to look for me?"

He watched her play with her spoon. "I wanted to see if I could help you find a job. You know, one artist to another, kind of thing. As a matter of fact," she lowered her spoon, "I talked with someone about you today."

"You're kidding, who?"

"Spencer Keith. He's the owner of New Hope Soup Kitchen."

She was serious. She was actually trying to find him work.

"Of course, he can't promise anything. You understand. But he said for you to come by next week. He may have something then."

"That's...thoughtful of him."

"At first, you might have to do some menial tasks, but you could write at night and submit your articles to some of the local newspapers or magazines."

He rested his forearms on the table and gazed at her.

She lifted the edge of his sleeve. "You'll need a few other things to wear besides this. The Goodwill store is a great resource. You wouldn't believe the nice things they have. You just have to look. I could meet you there if you'd like? There's one over on—"

"Thanks, but I can't."

Jill stared at him, forehead creased. "I don't understand."

"Thank you for the information. I'll take it from here."

She gnawed her lower lip. "You're not going to go, are you?"

"Probably not."

"You know, there's something about you and all of this that isn't quite kosher."

He took a bite of his sandwich, unable to look her in the eye.

"Please look at me," she said.

He swallowed and lifted his gaze to hers. "How so?"

"You smell too nice for one thing."

"In all my years, no one has ever said that to me."

"You know it's true."

"I do, huh?"

Talk about smelling nice. She leaned her pretty self toward him and it was all he could do not kiss her then and there. But he couldn't. Not as Phil.

"You're not like any homeless man I've ever met."

"I take it you've met your share?" he said.

"You'd be surprised. Who are you, really?" Her voice filled with a tender eagerness to know the answer.

"Just because you want something, doesn't make it so." He needed to end this now. He lifted the napkin from his lap and placed it on the table. "I'll tell you who I'm not. I'm not some stray dog who needs your attention."

The sparkling, inquisitive light faded from her eyes. He may as well have thrown cold water on her face. She blinked and sat back. Silence filled the space between them. Speechless, she stared at him, a myriad of emotions crossing her face.

She licked her lips. "You...you're right." She slowly pushed away from the table, stood and methodically shoved one arm, then the other, into her coat. "You're absolutely right. I'm a fool and an idiot. Your kind...they don't want help...until it's too late."

What the heck did that mean? He watched her, witnessed the rush of tears to her eyes and her valiant attempt to control the flow. He stood, just as she picked up the shopping bags.

"I'll see you to a cab."

"No." She whipped around. "I don't need your help. Whether you believe it or not, I can take care of myself."

She threw her arms out toward him. "Why don't you take care of your *own* self. You don't have to live like this. Especially when there's someone out there who wants to help you." She shook her head. "You don't even see it. Somebody out there loves you. Someone like your mom and you're breaking her heart. And all she wants is for you to come home."

A sob broke from her lips, and she rushed out, most likely believing she'd never see him again. But he knew differently.

CHAPTER FIFTEEN

The following day, Cameron arrived at the soup kitchen. He'd set up the interview with Spencer Keith mid-morning in order to beat the daily lunch line. He'd heard good things about the place from some of the homeless men in his circles and was surprised when Jill had mentioned it to *Phil* yesterday.

The simple one-story red brick building housed a ton of heart for the homeless in this part of town. He'd no sooner stepped through the entrance, when a hefty man with a friendly face approached him.

"You must be Cameron Phillips."

"I am."

"Spencer Keith, it's nice to meet you. Coffee?"

"Please."

He followed Spencer past several dining tables. Each one displayed a miniature Christmas centerpiece of greenery and ornaments. "Looks like you're ready for a party?"

"Not really. It's like this all December long. For some of these folks, it's all the Christmas they have."

Cam nodded. "I appreciate you seeing me on such short notice."

"Anything for Jill."

Cameron helped himself to the coffee craft, then took a seat opposite Spencer.

"I understand you help the homeless find work?"

"I do what I can, but it's not something that happens every day. Most of the work is manual labor, sweeping up, washing dishes, things like that. Sadly, some of the men and women I work with just aren't interested. They'd rather live on the streets. Between missions like mine and some of the others around the city, many of them are content." He lifted a hand. "A side effect of hopelessness."

Cam thought of the homeless people he knew, and realized there was some truth to Spencer's statement.

"Well, I happen to know one homeless man who might be interested in some work."

"Sure, send him over anytime."

After the meeting the two shook hands. "Give my best to Jill."

"About that. Jill doesn't know I'm here and I'd like to keep it that way… For the time being."

Spencer nodded.

"I'm concerned about her jaunts into not so friendly territory," Cam said.

"So, you know about that."

"I do. And I have to confess, I don't get it. She already works with teenage girls and yet she insists on being—"

"Reckless?"

Cam chuckled. "I guess."

"Well, she's not. Her interest with the homeless has to do with Steve. I guess she's told you about him."

"She mentioned him when we first met."

"See that photo collage on the wall behind me? Do you see Jill in any of the pictures?"

"Yes. Several." If someone had told him what he'd find here, he would never have believed it. Most of the photos of her were taken with one man. A man with wire-rimmed glasses, longish hair and a short, scruffy beard. The spitting image of *Phil*, twenty years from now.

Cam finally got it. Got her. He understood the *why* behind what he'd considered foolish actions, which weren't foolish at all, but heartfelt and noble.

"Jill started volunteering here three years ago, right after she moved to the city. As you can imagine, everyone here loved her. Steve wouldn't come in the building to eat and Jill decided to make him her special project. After three Sundays of working with him, she finally got him to come inside. That's him in the beard.

"In all my years, I've never seen anyone pour herself into another person like she did with Steve. Worked with him every Sunday for three months. Had even gotten him an interview for a good job, but when the time came for the meeting, he didn't show up. Two days later, the police found him dead in an alley."

"How did he die?"

"Overdose. Heroin."

"Good God."

"Jill never came back. Until, yesterday. I just hope this Phil guy turns out to be worth it."

CHAPTER SIXTEEN

Tuesday evening, Jill pushed open the entrance to a third-story building on West Thirty-Fourth Street and sprinted the steep stairway until she reached the top floor. The only marking on the door depicted a silhouette in a martial arts pose. The instructor, former NYPD officer David Walker, taught self-defense classes there twice a week.

Winded from the steep climb, she paused to catch her breath and glanced at her wristwatch. Maybe one day she'd actually make it on time.

When she entered the studio, the class was just starting. She tossed her gym bag in the corner and quickly joined the others on the floor.

After the class, David approached her. "Nice job tonight, Jill."

"Thank you." She bent over and grabbed a white towel from her gym bag.

"Are you ready to help me teach a class? You've been at this for almost a year and have been one of my most adept students. You're exceptional and your instincts are impeccable."

She wiped the last of her sweat, then tossed the towel back in the bag. "David, you know I only come to keep in shape and to practice self-defense. Plus, I really can't add another thing to my schedule right now. But," she shrugged into her oversized wool sweater and yanked it over her head, "I appreciate the confidence."

"A one-time presentation, then. Look, I have a guest coming to my Tuesday evening beginners group and I'd like for you to spar with him. He's a former student and will soon be teaching a high school group during the spring semester. Much of his class will be teenage girls."

"Why me?"

"You're exceptional at this and so is he. *And*, to keep him humble." He smiled. "I told him I had a diminutive, fireball student who could whip his butt."

She laughed. "And what did he say to that?"

"Bring it on."

Her smile faded. "Wait a minute." She folded her arms and gave him her best stare. "How do I know *I'm* not a target in your little scheme?"

He shrugged. "You don't."

Hands on hips, she asked, "What lesson do I need to learn?"

"Show up Tuesday and you'll see." He winked.

She stared at his departing figure. What had she just agreed to?

* * *

Cam arrived at Walker's self-dense class thirty minutes early. He'd enjoy the few quiet minutes before the rest of the group arrived.

David Walker entered the studio from a back entrance. "Getting yourself in the zone?"

"Yes. I figured I'd better stretch some before you turn this female ninja on me."

David laughed. "You're right about that."

When most of the students had arrived, David glanced at the door. "I just hope she hasn't changed her mind."

Cam was beginning to hope she would forget. He was as tough as anyone his size and fitness level, but David's praise of this young woman was starting to worry him. What if she *did* kick his butt? He'd never outlive it.

The class had gathered on the floor, quietly putting themselves through a series of warm up stretches.

Cam couldn't help but glance at the door for the firebrand's entrance. The wall clock said it was past time to begin. He looked over at David and shrugged. David shot back a look that said, you might have escaped this time, but there's always next week. He shook his head and started the class.

They had just finished the warm-up when a soft thud and the padding of bare feet tapped quickly across the wooden floor. David's raised brow and slight smile told Cam she had arrived.

Cam turned around and froze. The young woman approaching David was Jill Jeffrey. How was this possible? She was smiling at something David had said, then turned toward the group.

"This is the student I've been telling you all about. She's one of my graduates, but continues to come to my class to stay in shape and to keep vigilant in fine-tuning her method. I've invited her to spar with another one of my former graduates who will soon be teaching an all-girls self-defense class at one of our local high schools in the spring. "Most of you have already met Cameron. Cam, come up front and let's get this show going."

Jill's eyes grew wide and her formerly smiling lips parted in dismay. The horrified expression on her face as he approached her was priceless. So, little Miss JJ Designs could in fact take care of herself. Well, the next ten minutes would tell if that was indeed true or a fairy tale. David had been known to exaggerate and his raving of Jill's ability would be no exception.

"Jill, meet Cameron Phillips, your sparring partner for the evening. Cam, meet Jill."

Cam had no doubt David was enjoying the moment. If he only knew the history his two protégés actually shared.

Cam stuck out his hand. "Pleasure to meet you." He'd deliberately not revealed their connection, allowing her to divulge it if she chose.

Jill glanced from him to David. No doubt wondering if she should make known their relationship.

"And you," Jill said.

"Let's begin," David clapped his hands together. "There are three responses to being assaulted. One, you fight back. Which is the best response. Or, you fight back and run. That's also a good response. The third is you freeze. That's not good. Tonight's class focuses on the first and best response, fighting back. Cam and Jill will now demonstrate."

"Let's start with scenario one. Cam, approach Jill from behind and grab her around the waist with your right arm. Jill, what do you do?"

Without hesitation, Jill elbowed Cameron's ribs. Her action loosened Cam's arm. Jill spun and stepped away.

"As you can see, Jill's swift elbow action aided in her release."

That's the move she'd used on him in the subway. One of his ribs had hurt for an hour afterward.

"That's what you're aiming for." David continued. "If someone has you in their grasp, you first want to take action to get your release. The next response is either run for it or fight back. Many situations don't lend themselves to an easy get away. So, Cam place Jill in a choke hold position and Jill, show us what you'd each do next?"

Cam's hand barely touched her right shoulder when—

Whoosh, his back hit the floor. How the heck? He glanced at David who not only didn't try to stifle his grin, but stood, arms folded completely enjoying Cam's humiliation. You'd think the, *I told you so* gleam in David's eye would have been enough for his former instructor.

Chin raised, Jill stepped back. The class applauded. The winning light in her eye now motivated him.

Okay, fine. You can have round one, sweetheart.

Cam unfolded his long body off the mat and stood.

"Okay Cam, grab her wrist. Jill you're on."

Jill squatted down into a strong stance, leaned forward and bent her elbow until it reached his forearm, breaking Cam's hold.

David turned to his class. "Do you see how Jill used her full body here? She didn't just try to pull away from him."

Cam and Jill took another stance and stepped into the routine. This time, Cam blocked her effort and in four seconds effortlessly pinned her to his chest. Her heart fluttered like a wild bird against his forearm, making it difficult to concentrate. The top of her head hit his collarbone. He inhaled deeply to steady his own beating heart, breathing in the heady scent of her strawberry scented shampoo.

Jill sucked in air, blinked and stared, wide-eyed up at him. The beat of her heart against his arm matched his own. The quick rise and fall of her breasts against his torso made him want to keep holding her in that position. She was quick and savvy for sure, except when he was caught unaware. She'd be no match for someone like him.

As he held her, he knew he could break her in half and that frightened him for her. She was way too lax in where she went in the city. The thought of her getting hurt or worse compelled him to squeeze a bit tighter than he would have in any class demonstration. Something between a yelp and a squeak rushed from her parted lips and he released her.

* * *

Jill mentally berated herself for her treacherous heart. She'd been shocked to discover Cameron Phillips was to be her sparring partner. The past two weeks in his company had her wondering what it would feel like to have his arms around her. Well, now she knew.

Blood tingling torture—in a good way.

She swallowed against her dry mouth. His close proximity parched her throat and had her seeing stars. He had a dizzying effect on her nervous system. Heart pounding, she raised her hand to her throat, then took the pose and waited. She'd had him on the ground in seconds, but could tell by the look in his eye it would be the last time if he had anything to say about it.

Her legs were shaking. Not at all good if she was to have an inkling of success tonight. David put them through a few more self-defense moves for the students.

Just when she thought the demonstration was over, David said, "Now I want you to spar using your own wits."

Jill stared at Cam. It was hard to tell what he was thinking at that moment, but by the expression on his face, he wasn't pleased about it either.

"Whoever pins the other one wins. I'll time it for sixty seconds, if no one is pinned by then, it'll be a draw."

One minute. An eternity in something like this.

"I'll start you off." David handed Cam a plastic water pistol. "Jill, Cam has pulled a gun on you."

Cam pointed the plastic gun at her. Jill licked her lips and tried distraction. She glanced over his shoulder as if someone were behind him. He didn't take the bait. She clamped her teeth over her lower lip, looked over at David as if to say, this is not working. Cam also glanced at David and Jill took action. She grabbed Cam's wrist and twisted. But because of his height she couldn't get his gun hand low enough to snap the weapon away. Cam used his other arm and swung her body to his chest. With her back to him, Jill threw both arms apart. For a second she was free. She started to run, but Cam tackled her, bringing them both down on the mat. Jill scurried to her feet. Cam grabbed the sensitive spot below her ankle and squeezed. She yelped and collapsed to the mat. Before she could get back up, Cam spread his legs over her body, grabbed her arms and pinned her.

Back flat, arms pinned overhead, she stared into his eyes, breathless, gulping air. Cam didn't move but held her in that position for several long seconds, his forehead glistening with beads of sweat. She made one last attempt to break his hold and pushed against his weight, but without success. She swallowed and licked her lips.

Somewhere in the distance she heard David speak. "Cam is our winner. Get up you two." Mild laughter and light applause seeped into her brain. Cam stood and put his hand out to assist her. Clasping a firm grip, he pulled her to her feet.

After the class dispersed, David shook hands with Jill, then Cam. "You guys were great. I hope you had as much fun as the rest of us.

"Happy to help," Cam said.

"What did you think of Jill, Cam? Everything I said about her true?"

Cam gave a lopsided grin and nodded. "I have to confess I'm pleasantly surprised."

"Since you've never sparred with a female, I wanted you to work with Jill. You're a tough guy. Because of that you need to manage your strength with your female students."

"Got it."

David turned to Jill. "And I hope you now realize that even with your skill, fighting a man who's twice your size in a controlled situation is just that. Controlled. What happens if you meet some thug in one of these tent cities?"

"They're not all thugs."

"I'll concede that, but what about the ones who are? I'm aware of where you go in this town. And it concerns me."

She rubbed her hip. "Point taken."

CHAPTER SEVENTEEN

Cam pulled on his sweats and jacket and waited while Jill slipped into hers. Her instincts on the mat were impressive, but like David, he too worried about her visits alone to the tent cities. As he watched her slip on her fleece jacket, the action brought to mind the previous day—when teary-eyed-Jill shrugged into her coat, before rushing out of the bistro. He still felt badly about hurting her feelings.

When Jill finished dressing, they walked out together. The air had grown sharp and he zipped his jacket higher.

"You pack a mean punch," he said.

Jill cut her eyes in his direction and smiled. "So do you."

"I've worked up an appetite. You hungry?"

"Yeah, sure. I could eat something."

They found a hole-in-the-wall Italian café nearby and went in. The open-seating sign stood in the entrance, so they made their way to a small red and white checked covered table in the far left corner. Cam shook out the large white napkin onto his lap and lifted the menu.

They both ordered meatballs and spaghetti. Cam chose a red wine to complement the meal and Jill went with iced tea.

"What made you take up martial arts?" Cam asked.

"My parents were concerned about me living alone in New York. After some discussion, I agreed to take self-defense classes. At first it was simply to ease their minds, but after my first class I was hooked."

"So, how often do you visit our tent cities?"

Her eyes filled with annoyance. "I've only been there once or twice." She shrugged. "Twice too many according to some."

He bit back a smile. "At the risk of sounding chauvinistic, David's right. That's not a place for a woman alone."

"Who says I went alone?"

He cocked a brow.

She pursed her soft lips. "The first time I did and the second I took someone with me."

He thought about the young man, no more than a teenager, who he'd seen with her. He shook his head.

"What? You don't believe me?"

"Of course I believe you."

The waiter showed up with hot bread and butter, then left.

"Why go there?" he asked. "It's rather an odd place to be hanging around."

"I didn't *hang*. I was looking for someone."

"In a tent city?"

"Yes. In a tent city." She was openly annoyed.

"Let me guess. This is the same person we talked about last week. The one you were trying to find."

"Yes."

"Any luck with the police?"

"I haven't gone to the police."

"Why?"

"What would I say? That I met this man who lives on the street? He's tall with a short beard, wears glasses and I know his first name is Phil. I can hear them now, 'Lady, that describes ninety percent of all the homeless men in this city.' They would laugh me out of the station."

"You know. As a man, I would imagine this Phil person is capable of taking care of himself. My advice. Let it go. Let *him* go."

"I know. I should."

"But…you won't."

And like Sister Mary Margaret from middle school, she leaned into the table and pinned him with her forthright gaze. "The last time I was with him, we were having a sandwich at a bistro near the park. He pretty much told me in no uncertain terms to get lost." She slumped back in her chair. "I have no idea if I'll ever see him again."

"And you? What did you say?"

She licked her lips and squeezed a lemon wedge into her tea. "Some things I now regret."

"Were they true?"

She lifted her head and looked at him. "Yes."

"Then you have nothing to feel badly about."

"Why do some men have trouble parking their pride? You know, not accepting help."

"Maybe it depends on who's offering. Some men do have trouble. Sometimes it's pride, but sometimes it's because they believe they can take care of themselves."

"But what if the person is in a desperate situation? How do you convince him he doesn't have to stay there?"

"People can be stubborn. And may I just add, and forgive me for saying this, but I think it's crazy to chase after this man. He could be a criminal for all you know."

"I'm not chasing him. It's not like that. I hurt him, but now it's not even that really."

"Then what is it?"

"It's personal. At least it started out that way. But as I've talked with him… He's not… I mean… I'm not convinced he's homeless. The guy's educated, articulate—"

"Do you realize how many educated men and women are homeless?"

She slapped her hand on the table. "That's exactly what he said."

After dinner, they entered the street near the bus stop. "Thanks for dinner, but you didn't have to pick up the tab."

"It's the least I could do after that licking I gave you tonight."

"Dream on—" Jill paused mid-step and lifted a finger. "Just a second." She hurried over to a woman seated at the bus stop. She was holding a large quilted shoulder bag in her lap.

"Excuse me, but where did you get that?" Jill asked.

The woman shifted her eyes right, then looked down at the bag. "I found it."

"Where exactly?"

The woman shrugged. "I don't know."

Jill folded her arms and bent over the woman.

The move seemed rather intimidating, and so unlike Jill. Cam placed a hand on her arm. "Jill, maybe you should—"

Jill shot him her Sister Mary Margaret glare that told him in no uncertain terms to be quiet.

He chewed his inner lip and waited, while Jill turned her attention back to the woman.

"You have two choices… You can either tell me or the police."

"Take it." She rolled her eyes and handed the bag to Jill. "There's nothing but junk in there anyway."

Jill took the bag, but when the woman refused to say more, Jill pulled her phone from her sweats and held it up. "One last chance."

"Fine. There's an old woman, around the corner in the alley. I got it from her."

"When?"

"Ten, fifteen minutes ago."

Jill took off for the corner. Cam followed, catching up with her a few seconds later.

"What's that all about?"

"Come on. I'll explain later."

They turned at the alley and, sitting on the ground, propped against the brick building, sat an elderly woman.

"Miss Adele!" Jill broke into a run.

In seconds she was down on her knees beside the slumped body.

Miss Adele lifted her head. She wasn't as old as Cam had first thought and looked to be in her mid-to-late sixties.

"Oh, my gosh." Jill placed her hands on either side of the woman's face. "Miss Adele. Are you okay? What happened?"

The older woman blinked and gripped Jill's arm. "Jill? Is that you?"

"Yes, yes. Where are your glasses?"

"I fell. I don't know."

"It's okay. We'll get you another pair." She glanced at Cam, eyes pleading. "Help me get her to her feet."

Cam bent, looped his arms underneath Miss Adele and lifted. Jill grabbed the lady's other side and the two of them steadied the woman on her feet.

"Miss Adele, this is my friend Cameron Phillips. He and I are going to take you to New Hope, okay."

"Okay."

Twenty minutes later they pushed through the entrance of the soup kitchen.

"Miss Adele! We've been worried about you." Bret hurried over, looking to Jill for an explanation.

"We found her on the street. She fell and she's also lost her glasses."

"We'll make sure she gets a new pair."

"From the looks of her, I'd say she hasn't been here in a while," Jill said.

Bret nodded. "Two months, at least."

Adele's hand trembled as she grabbed Jill's hand. "I couldn't find the street."

"It's going to be okay." Jill patted her shoulder. "Bret will make sure you get a new pair of glasses, then you'll be right as rain."

"Does she need a doctor?" Cam asked.

"We have a volunteer nurse who comes when we need her. I'll call, then get Miss Adele something to eat."

"Jill."

Jill swung around. "Peter McNally." She took both his hands in hers. "Last time I saw you, you'd gotten a job. How's that going?"

"Not too well. The warehouse downsized."

"Oh, no."

Jill listened intently, nodding when appropriate as Peter told his story.

In between her fan party, Cam asked, "How in the world did you know the shoulder bag was Miss Adele's?"

"Because I made it for her."

"Oh."

A petite woman approached Jill from behind and tapped her on the shoulder.

"Winnie!"

Jill threw her arms around the tiny African American woman, who wasn't much bigger than Jill.

"We've all missed you, Jill."

"I've missed you, too."

He stood aside as Jill walked the lady to a seat at the dining table. Jill's interaction with these people continued to amaze him.

Kind, attentive, and respectful.

The embodiment of everything the disadvantaged needed. And yet in a moment of anger and through his own false assumptions, he'd placed a target on her back. Pointed a disapproving finger when applause would have been much more appropriate.

Tonight, Jill had surprised the heck out of him. Far from the silly, do-gooder socialite he'd first thought. She knew these people and they adored her.

He knew from his own experience with the homeless that you don't build these types of relationships on the fly. At some point, Jill had invested in each of their lives. He rubbed his hand over his jaw.

In that moment, she looked up as if she'd been aware of his scrutiny. Her lips parted in a sunny smile. Bright, happy, and glowing. He couldn't help, but smile back.

No doubt about it, Jill had a gift. Most people wouldn't give these people the time of day much less hours week after week.

No wonder Phil had captured Jill's interest in a way Cam had not understood. But, Cameron Phillips could offer her so much more. He knew in that moment he would do his best to get to know her. No more prejudging. No more suspicions. He would accept her for who she was and promised himself he'd enjoy the journey in that discovery.

This complex, adorable, petite young woman housed a multitude of layers and he planned to unearth every single one. She was suddenly the most irresistible creature he'd ever known. In spite of that first negative impression all he'd seen since that day was a young woman with heart. Genuine, thoughtful, the real deal and he'd be crazy to let her get away.

He stuffed his hands deep into his pockets. He just hoped his past actions hadn't sabotaged their relationship or their future.

Chapter Eighteen

Wednesday morning Jill sat at her desk finalizing the last of the sketches for Sloan's Back-to-School line. She slid the finished drawing across the desk for Amy's perusal. "What do you think?"

"I love them," Amy said. "And so will Sloan's."

"Let's get mock-ups done by next Monday. I'll set up a showing for the buyer on the following Tuesday afternoon."

Amy held up both hands with her fingers crossed. "This is big, Jill. I'm rooting for you."

"Thanks."

After Amy left, Jill pulled her laptop from her tote bag and set it on the desk. She typed in Eagle Eye dot com to see if he'd written anything else since the homeless piece came out. She'd checked weekly, but he hadn't posted anything in over a month.

She shut the computer and sat back. She'd hoped to find another one, something that could help give her a clue to the Eagle's identity. She wondered again how the man had learned about her on the night of the fundraiser. Had he been watching her? The image of a bird of prey rose in her mind's eye, circling overhead for the next unsuspecting rodent. No wonder he called himself The Eagle. She shivered. He had to have been there. Most likely one of the reporters covering the event.

She opened her computer and did a Google search of the gala. Four news media outlets came up. Each one had done a feature story on the event. She scrolled through the entire list, clicking on each one. One magazine, two newspapers and one local TV station reported on it. But, no one from the *Post*. How could that be? Unless he sold the story to them. She went back through each outlet present and searched the editors involved. Here was something. *Beverly Blake formerly of the New York Post has now joined the Week End News.*

So Beverly was with the *Post*? She might know the Eagle Eye's identity. Jill picked up the office phone and dialed.

* * *

As luck would have it, Beverly was happy to meet with Jill and had a small opening in her schedule that afternoon.

"Jill, it's nice to meet you. Please take a seat."

"Thanks." Jill shook Beverly's hand.

"Can I get you something to drink? Coffee, water?"

"No, I'm good."

Beverly sat back and folded her hands in her lap. "How can I help you?"

"This is going to sound odd, but do you know the identity of the Eagle Eye? He writes for the *Post*."

"I know, but I don't know who he is. I'm sorry."

"Someone must know? I mean, how is he paid?"

"Most likely his editor."

"So he's not necessarily a New Yorker?"

"That's right." She shrugged. "But then again he could be."

"I see."

"Have you tried checking his bio?"

"Yes, but there's nothing there either."

"May I ask, why?"

"There's a mistake in his most recent story."

"It must be pretty substantial for you to go to these lengths to find him."

Jill nodded.

"Have you considered writing a response? Newspapers always have a section for rebuttals or responses to their articles."

Actually she had, but knew a response would only confirm her identity to her colleagues. "A friend of mine suggested the same thing to me."

"Well, there you go then. And you never know, it might help to clear things up."

"I'll give it some thought." Jill stood and shook Beverly's hand. "Thank you for your time."

A few minutes later, Jill pushed through the revolving door to the street just as Cam was coming in.

* * *

Cam stopped and waited when he saw her.

"Hi," Jill said. "Is this where you work?"

"No, I have an appointment. So, what are you doing here?"

"A bit of investigating."

"Really?"

She nodded.

"Are you sore?"

"Very." She pointed her index finger at him. "And you'd better be, too."

He laughed. "I am."

"Well, I need to get going. It was nice seeing you." She turned to leave.

"Hey, how's Miss Adele?"

"Much better. I talked with Bret this morning. She should have a new pair of glasses in a day or two."

"That's great."

She nodded and chewed her bottom lip.

Why did he suddenly feel like a high school freshman? Sweaty palms and all. "The girls at the home are looking forward to our visit on Saturday."

"Great. I can't wait. I've planned a fabulous day for them. Including lots of gifts."

"Good. Well, I guess I'll see you on Saturday."

"Eight a.m. I'll be waiting."

* * *

Cameron walked to the elevator. Just as it was about to close, he sprinted forward, throwing his arm into the opening.

He got off on the third floor and headed to Beverly Blake's office.

"Good afternoon, Bev. Congrats on the new job."

"Thanks." They shook hands. "I love not having to work nights. I've just fixed a coffee, would you like one?"

"No thanks." He took a seat across from her desk.

"Hey, you don't happen to know the identity of the Eagle Eye, do you?"

He lifted a brow. "That's out of left field."

"I know. There was a young lady here earlier who wanted to know if I knew who he was."

Jill.

"Oh yeah?"

"Someone named Jill Jeffrey."

"I know Jill. I ran into her on my way in. What'd she say, exactly?"

"That the Eagle Eye had the facts wrong in his last article. I don't know who he is, but he packs quite a punch when he wants to." She sat back like the proverbial cat that swallowed the canary. "Like someone else I know."

"What is that supposed to mean?" He gave her his most bland expression. "You don't seriously think it's me?"

"No. I don't. I've known you a long time. I've never known you to put any name on your articles, but your own. Your research is impeccable."

Except when it came to Jill.

"No one else is getting the credit for your work, not even a pretend you. Right?"

"That's true. I'm way too arrogant."

"So tell me about the story idea?" she asked. "You said it was about a merger."

"That's right. Time Warner and AT&T."

"I'm on it. I'll set up an interview for you with David Cummings at Warner. Or…" Beverly brightened. "I know you hate these things, but why don't you meet me tonight at the Hollisters' Annual Christmas party. Cummings should be there. I can introduce you, then."

He nodded and stood. "Fine."

"They live in Scarsdale," she said.

"I know where they live."

She cocked a plucked brow. "Good, then you won't need directions."

He left her office, promising he'd be at the party. If nothing else, at least his mother—a socialite of the first order—would be pleased.

Normally, he wouldn't be hounding his friends in the industry for work, but since his investment in Apalacha Key's newspaper he had to write the occasional fluff article. He considered the Like No Other article fluff. Get in, get out and get paid, but he hadn't reckoned on meeting Jill again, much less shadowing her for two weeks.

He pushed through the revolving door onto the busy street and was met with throngs of New Yorkers. And now he discovered Jill was doing some research of her own.

Good luck with that, sweetheart. Even the professionals in his industry hadn't discovered the Eagle's identity.

As he wove his way through the crowded sidewalk he wondered how she'd chosen Beverly Blake to question. Remarkable girl, Jill. It seemed self-preservation ran in her blood. He couldn't fault her for that. He knew she was trying to protect her identity. Why else would she search out a former colleague of his from the *Post*?

Since his eye-opening talk with Spencer Keith, he'd learned a few things about her that had him wishing he'd never referred to her in his article.

How could the young woman Spencer had told him about turn around and use a homeless man the way she had? Of course, she'd had no idea she'd get caught. Phil was not supposed to find out. He was supposed to leave the gala fed and none the wiser. LNO would get a whopping donation and Jill would qualify for the board position. No harm, no foul.

Except Phil did find out and Cameron included the ruse in his article. Her motives had never been to hurt Phil or anyone else.

He pulled his collar up against the wind and strode down the street. He wondered if he should just come right out and tell her who he was and that he'd written the article. Apologize for any harm he may have done to her and her career.

Remorse filled him. His article had hurt her more than he'd realized. Jill was a sweet naïve young woman, really. The night of the gala she'd made a mistake. It was that simple. He knew that now. Knew she'd never intentionally hurt anyone. He'd continue to hang around in hopes to lessen the blow. And in his business, he knew the blow would most definitely come. It was only a matter of time.

* * *

Friday afternoon, Jill stood to the side of six form-fitting mannequins, which displayed the prototype for her new line of spring clothing for Sloan's. The buyer, Liz Fuller, stepped around the last one finishing up her inspection.

"Fantastic, Jill."

"Here's the full-scale diagram for the rest of the designs," Jill said.

"Wonderful. You can expect an order in a day or so."

"Thank you, Liz."

After Liz left, Amy squealed and Jill danced a jig. Then Amy looped her arm through Jill's and they danced around the mannequins until they were out of breath.

"Can you believe it?" Amy panted. "Sloan's just ordered your designs. For *all* of their stores."

"I know." Jill placed her hands against her thumping heart. "I keep thinking I'll wake up and realize it was all a dream."

"Do you know what this means?"

"Paychecks for all and then some," Jill said. "We'll be able to bring on two, maybe three more seamstresses because of this account."

"This is just the beginning. Once your line is in their stores, others will follow. There will be fashion shows, news articles—"

"Full color ads in the latest teen magazines."

"Soon, celebrities will be wearing JJ. Designs."

"And then, my own line of boutiques."

"All across the county."

"The world!"

Jill and Amy laughed, hugged, then laughed some more.

"This calls for celebration." Amy ran to the kitchen and returned a minute later with sparkling water and two coffee mugs.

Amy poured while Jill held the cups. "To JJ Designs."

They tapped the rims and drank.

Chapter Nineteen

The drive to the boarding school took about an hour. Once outside the city the scenery turned to rolling green hills and massive hardwood trees.

"It's beautiful here," Jill said. "I sometimes forget how pretty the state is. I get that nose-to-the-grind stone thing going and forget to look up for days."

"I know," Cam said. "I'm so used to concrete and tall buildings everywhere I look. I really haven't thought that much about it. It's where I grew up. The only time I see green is when I'm jogging in the park."

"I didn't realize you grew up in the city."

"I was originally from Scarsdale and after my parents' divorce I moved into town with my father."

Maybe that's why he disliked Scarsdale. Something from his past, maybe.

"That's tough. How old were you?"

"Fifteen. How about your family. What are they like?"

"You've heard of the old TV show, Ozzie and Harriet?"

"The perfect family. You were lucky."

"I still am."

Maybe it was time she let down her guard with Cam. Time to tell him who she really was. A Jeffrey of Paige Point. Or would he also dump her if he discovered she was *a nobody* from Maryland? Not that there was anything to dump. They weren't even dating.

"And we're here," he said.

After they parked, Cameron carried Jill's poster, while Jill managed the heavy tote bag.

Margaret Simms, the housemother, met them at the front entrance.

"Margaret, meet Jill Jeffrey."

Margaret clasped Jill's hand. "We're so happy you could come." She led them down a wide, walnut-paneled hallway.

"This house is amazing," Jill said. "Forgive my saying so, but the upkeep on this place must be enormous."

Margaret smiled. "It can be. The last owner of the Bell Estate left it in trust to be used as an orphanage/boarding school for girls ages six to eighteen. Donations play a huge part in the upkeep, as well."

They turned left and entered a small conference-like room on the first floor. "The Bell Home for Children is now home to forty young ladies," Margaret said. "The youngest here is eleven and the oldest is seventeen. You'll be meeting some of them shortly."

"I can't wait."

"Neither can the girls. They've talked of nothing else since I told them you were coming."

* * *

Cam helped Jill set up the room, then stood behind the snack table serving punch to each girl as they entered. Then he saw her . . .

She looked nothing like the dirty-faced urchin from the tent city—hair all clean and pulled back with a shiny barrette. Dressed like the other girls at the home, she wore a white blouse, plaid skirt and knee socks with black and white saddle oxfords.

Looking at her now, one would never know she'd lived on the streets of New York City. To say this was a proud moment for him was putting it mildly. He watched her with all the fondness of an adoring uncle and wished he could reveal his identity to her. But seeing her happy and safe would have to do.

As she approached the snack table, he ladled the pink brew into a cup and handed it to her. "Hi, there. What's your name?"

"Lisa." She cradled the cup in one hand and grabbed a cookie with her other.

So her name *was* Lisa.

She thanked him, clueless as to his identity. Not surprising. Phil with his longish hair, rimmed eyeglasses and beard looked nothing like the clean-shaven, short haired, well-dressed man serving punch. Not even Jill could tell them apart.

"Nice to meet you, Lisa. This is a pretty swanky place, huh?"

"Yeah."

"How do you like living here?"

"I love it so much."

She gazed at him, her expression sincere and relaxed. He was happy to see her frightened-rabbit look had disappeared. Immensely touched, he ladled the punch into a cup and handed it to her. "Enjoy."

"Um, I already have a cup."

"Ah, yes you do. Sorry about that."

She smiled up at him seemingly without a care in the world. He smiled back, then watched her take a seat next to a blonde teen, chatting and giggling like girls were supposed to do at that age. It felt good to see her here. Surrounded by people who cared. Knowing she had a real chance now.

After all the girls arrived and got settled, he took his spot near the back of the room. As usual, Jill amazed, entertained, and taught with humor and honesty. By the end of the day, she'd gained each girl's trust and adoration.

After all the hugs and goodbyes, he and Jill sailed down the highway in his BMW.

"What a great day." Jill turned in her seat. "Thank you for setting this up."

"That part was easy, you did all the work."

"Nothing about this day has been work. I had more fun with this group than with any I can remember."

"Why is that, do you think?"

A pensive expression crossed her features. "Maybe it's because they appreciate it the most."

An hour later, Cameron walked Jill up the steps to her brownstone. When they reached the door she pulled the key from her purse and turned to him. "Would you like to come in for a drink?"

Had he heard her correctly? Was Jillian Jeffrey asking him to come inside? The temperature had dropped significantly since the sun had gone down, adding a rosy glow to her cheeks. The side door lights only enhanced it and her beauty. Her smile as she gazed at him was pleasant and sincere.

"I'd like that. Thanks."

She slid in the key and turned the handle, unlocking the massive door. Once inside, he followed her to the living room.

She set the tote bag just inside the door and nodded to the poster tucked under his arm. "Just put that down wherever you want."

The high ceiling room was filled with white linen-upholstered furniture and several antiques. Everything from the lamps to the art on the wall was the picture of old money and the establishment. The place had family money written all over it.

"What do you think? Nice, isn't it?"

She seemed perfectly at home surrounded by expensive things. As those with money usually did.

"It is, indeed. How long have you lived here?"

"A little over a year now."

"How did you manage to accumulate all this stuff in so short a time?"

"Oh, it's not mine."

"Seriously? I thought you owned all this."

"Nope. I'm house-sitting for a man who has a two-year gig in London."

She pointed to a bar in the far corner of the room. "Please help yourself. I'll just be a moment."

As Cam shrugged out of his jacket, he wondered what else he *didn't* know about Jill. The more he learned about her the more confused he became. "Can I fix you anything?" he asked.

"Perrier over ice with a lime." She shot over her shoulder as she left the room. A moment later, Cam heard the distant click of a door, then silence.

When she returned, he handed her the drink, then took a seat by the fireplace. "I took the liberty of lighting it while you were gone. Hope you don't mind."

"Not at all."

She kicked off her shoes, then curled up on the chair opposite. Sipping her drink, she tucked her bare feet underneath her. There was something intimate about the action and he wondered if she'd sensed it as well. A few strands of her hair had come lose during the drive back adding to her devil-may-care charm. Totally relaxed and sure of herself, he wondered about the change in her attitude toward him. Maybe it was simply the fact that she was at home.

"Do you play?" He lifted his tumbler, pointing it at the chessboard. "Or is that purely decoration?"

"I do, actually. Do you?"

"I sure do." He set his glass aside. "I see the board is already set up. Shall we?"

She responded with a bright smile and helped him move the square table between them.

"I haven't played in ages."

"White goes first and that's you," she said.

Cam jumped his knight over the pawn, then over one. Jill did the same on her side. After Cam moved one of his pawns, Jill did the same. The game progressed in an amiable fashion, neither really focused on the game as much as on each other. Fifteen minutes later, Cam had captured seven of her pieces, whereas she'd only gotten four of his.

Jill shook her head. "This is not going well for me."

"I'd have to agree." He moved his knight and took one of her rooks.

"Oh, man. Not my rook."

He smiled at her deflated expression. "You still have another one."

Jill chewed the inside of her lip, contemplating her next move.

"Who taught you to play?" he asked.

"A man named Steve."

His head shot up. "Steve?"

"Uh, huh. Three years ago, when I first came to the city."

"Tell me about him." Cam watched her closely. He'd been extremely interested in Jill's relationship with Steve since he'd heard a bit of their story from Spencer.

"He was a homeless man. We met at the soup kitchen." She moved a pawn up two. "And in case you hadn't already figured it out, I used to volunteer there on Sundays."

"I did notice." He chuckled.

"The first time I saw Steve he was sitting outside on the curb in front of the soup kitchen. Shoulders slumped, dead-eyed. He didn't like to come inside to eat, so I'd fix a plate and take it out to him."

He moved a pawn up one square.

"I usually timed my work so I could sit outdoors with him while he finished."

"How did chess come up?"

"One Sunday he offered a chess piece as payment for my kindness. It was a king. Hand carved. A beautiful piece. He told me I had treated him like one and that he wanted me to have it to remember him by."

"What a nice gesture."

"Yeah. He was genuinely kind. I thanked him and told him I'd always wanted to learn to play. You know, just making polite conversation. So, he asked me to meet him the following Tuesday in Central Park."

She captured one of his bishops and set it aside.

"Told me he would teach me. I asked the kitchen manager if he thought I should go. He said the chess area was a famous spot in the park—high traffic and very safe."

"So you went," Cam said.

"I did. For over two months. We sat at the same table, under the same shade tree, every Tuesday at three o'clock."

"That's remarkable."

"I discovered he was a highly intellectual, complex person."

She studied the board as she spoke.

"Had to be to play chess like he did. He taught me to study the endgame."

"To play the game in such a way so the pieces left at the end are just where you want them."

"Exactly." She gazed at the board and frowned. "A lot of good that's doing me now. Oh, wait, what's this?" She gave him a teasing look and smiled sweetly. "Checkmate."

"I…did not see that coming."

"Had you going, didn't I? Admit it. You didn't think I could really play."

He chuckled. "Well done."

"Thank you."

"So, why only three months?" Cam watched her closely. "What happened?"

Her smile faded. "He…died."

"And you don't like to talk about it."

She shook her head. "I followed him to the edge of a tent city. It was getting dark. I stood at the entrance, terrified to go farther and just watched him disappear into the crowd." She lifted her gaze to his. "I'd never seen so many miserable looking people. Glazy-eyed, and hopeless." She swallowed. "That was the last time I saw him. The police said it was an overdose. I thought he'd quit, but apparently not."

"I'm sorry." Her motivation to help Phil became even clearer. Phil, who'd been cavalier and frankly unworthy of her heart.

A tear escaped, then another and she quickly brushed them away. "If I'd just followed him. Maybe—"

"You don't know that."

Sniffing, she jumped up and walked over to a round table filled with several framed photos. After selecting one from the center, she sat back down.

"Here's one of him holding a trophy. I found it on the Internet."

Cam took the photo and held it underneath the lamp by his chair. "He's young here. This looks like a long time ago."

She nodded. "He'd been a chess prodigy in his youth. No telling where he could have ended up had his life gone differently."

Her sadness over the plight of this man shamed him after what he'd thought of her efforts to help Phil.

"My friends thought I was crazy meeting a homeless man in Central Park. I admit I've done some foolish things, but that wasn't one of them."

"Like going to abandoned subway stations."

"Yeah, like that."

"Where I take it you've tried to help someone else like him." Maybe this was his chance to get her to share about Phil.

She sniffed and nodded. "Except he didn't want my help, then for a completely different reason all of my efforts backfired."

"No good deed goes unpunished," he said, assuming she'd referred to his article.

Jill rested her tear-stained cheek in her hand and locked her gaze with his. "I wonder why that is?"

"I wish I knew."

She took the photo from his hand and set it on the side table. "If you only knew how many days I wished I'd been a big, tall man."

"If you had been, what would you have done differently?"

"Gone places where a petite female dare not." She rolled her eyes.

"You think you could have done more as someone else?"

"Possibly."

"So, you became a kick-ass ninja instead." He hated to see her cry. Wondered if she also cried for Phil. Shame engulfed him.

"I guess I did." She laughed through her tears. "And as I recall I kicked yours pretty well."

"I seem to remember that as more of a tie. That is until I pinned your backside on the mat."

"Go ahead and gloat if it makes you feel better." Chuckling, she took one last swipe at her cheeks. "I'm sorry. It usually takes a lot to make me cry. I don't know what's come over me."

God help him, she was the most beautiful creature this side of heaven. And with the most precious heart he'd ever encountered in a human being. Suddenly drawn to her in a way he'd never experienced before, he took both her hands and held them to his lips.

"You have a great heart, Jillian Jeffrey. Don't ever lose that." He thought about his article and the harshness of his words when describing her actions. Now that he knew the truth, he was completely outraged with himself that he'd included her in it. There had been much more to the story, had he but searched for it. His haste and anger in that moment was no excuse for not doing his job. Deadline or not. He'd known better. But, so far, to his knowledge, the article hadn't hurt her company. For that he was thankful, but he had to ask…

"How's your business?"

"Um." She tilted her head, as if questioning his abrupt change in subject. "It's okay. I'm having to manage a few unexpected bumps, but that's normal."

He nodded. "I should go. Will you be all right?"

"Yes, of course." She stood and brushed her hands down her thighs.

Cam shrugged into his coat.

"Look. Before you go, there's something I should tell you."

This sounded serious. He sucked in a breath and waited.

Her delicate brows pulled together. "I'm not a Scarsdale Jeffrey."

Relief flooded to his very bones. Her serious expression had put him on full alert.

"Is that right?" He smiled. "Then what Jeffrey are you?"

"A Jeffrey of Paige Point, Maryland."

"Who the heck are they?"

"Exactly!" She threw up her hands.

The humor of the situation wasn't lost on him. "It seems my assumption that you're a Jeffrey of Scarsdale has offended you."

"Trust me, you're not the first."

"Why didn't you tell me before?"

"Stubborn, I guess. And…I kind of enjoyed leading you on after your somewhat rude behavior—"

"Okay, okay. I apologize. For everything."

"Apology accepted." A slow smile spread across her upturned face.

He tipped her chin with his finger. "But, something tells me I've been missing out on *not* having known the Jeffreys of Paige Point."

She tilted her head. "That could be rectified."

"Is that a green light?" He stepped closer.

Her eyes grew enormous. "I…well…"

"Come on." He took her hand. "Walk me to the door."

They stopped at the entrance and Cam released her. "For the record, I'm extremely thankful you're not a big, tall man."

He gently placed his hands on each side of her head. Cupping her cheeks, he tilted her face toward his. He'd wanted to kiss her since the night he'd put her in the taxi as Phil. And she'd just given him the green light, so…he lowered his mouth to hers. Tentative. Exploring, savoring the warmth of her sweet lips. A rush of heat seared Cam to his core. Pulse quickening, he lowered his hands and encircled Jill in his arms. The scent of rose petals nearly threatened his resolve until his senses returned and he released her.

He lifted his head. "I'm sorry, I shouldn't have—"

"No, it's all right." She licked her lips and continued to stare at him. "In case you hadn't noticed, our two weeks are up," she blurted out.

"I know."

She licked her lips. "You can't need more for your article."

"Never said I did." He tweaked a strand of her hair. "Is it really that impossible to think I'd like to spend more time with you?"

She glanced at the floor then back at him. A twinkle lit her eyes. "I'd like to spend more time with you, too."

CHAPTER TWENTY

Sun pealed through the gap in the curtain hitting Jill smack in the face. She squinted, rubbed the crick in her neck and sat up. Glancing sleepily around the room, she lifted her fingers to her mouth. Cameron Phillips had kissed her. The night before she'd had so much trouble falling asleep. Cam's kiss had haunted her thoughts and in a totally good way.

Thinking about that kiss had her wondering where this relationship with Cam could be heading. And for the life of her, why did she have to go and cry like that? She never cried.

"Nothing worse to a man than a sniveling woman." She stomped to the bathroom. At least that's what she'd always heard. Not from her wonderful dad of course, but from men like Mark.

Maybe Cam was different. He'd treated her so sweetly. Not at all like she'd imagined he'd be with a woman. There was definitely a connection between them, a certain something that made her want to tell him everything.

Giddy goose bumps skipped over her flesh. Mark's kisses had never made her heart flutter like Cam's had. As her mind lingered on that kiss, one thing was certain. One wasn't nearly enough.

On her way to the kitchen, she halted mid-step and frowned. What if Cam had been merely comforting her? And that was all the kiss had meant. She groaned. Why else would he have apologized? You don't say you're sorry for kissing someone unless you hadn't really wanted to. But then, he did say he wanted to spend more time with her.

Jill second-guessed the kiss and Cameron's motives all the way to her office. Amy and the others had already arrived and… Oh, my, gosh…so had Cameron.

* * *

"Good morning?"

"Hi."

"Is it okay that I'm here? You don't look too pleased."

"Oh, no. It's fine. I just wasn't expecting to see you so…soon."

"I wanted you to see my article on LNO before it went to print." He handed her a hard copy. "Read it and if you have any suggestions or thoughts add them in the margin."

"Oh. Okay." She glanced at the document. "Right now?"

"No, sometime in the next day or so is fine."

"Jill." Amy approached them. "Could I see you in your office?"

"Sure." Jill turned to him. "As much as I'd love to stay here and visit…"

"I hear you. Text me when you're done and we'll grab lunch."

From the look on Amy's face he could tell Jill was about to be hit with some not-so-good news. "Do you mind if I grab a coffee before I go."

"Of course not." She lifted his article. "I'll get back with you on this."

After he fixed his to-go cup, he took his time making his way back to the front. He could see Amy and Jill through the glass partition. From the looks on their faces something was wrong. At that moment, Jill walked out of her office. She halted when she saw him.

"Everything okay?"

She shook her head. "It's a misunderstanding with a client."

"Sloan's?"

"Yes."

"I hope it's not too serious."

She hesitated as if gathering her thoughts. "I'm sure we'll work it out."

"You don't seem too certain of that." He hoped to God it wasn't the result of his article.

"It's just one of those things. Part of owning a business." She offered something close to a smile, but it fell flat.

"Anything I can do?"

"No." She glanced at the women already at work. "I need to check on them. Was there something else?"

"I was hoping you could take the afternoon off. There's something I'd like to talk with you about."

"I could leave around three, if that's not too late."

"No. That's perfect."

"Should we meet in the lobby, then?"

"Yes and thanks for the coffee."

Cam left JJ Designs and made his way to the elevator. From the anxiety reflected in Jill's eyes, her problem was bigger than she was letting on.

* * *

At three-fifteen Cam ushered Jill into a little bakery in the village. "Their lattes are fantastic and they have the most amazing pastries. I'm partial to the caramel scones."

"Say no more," Jill said.

"Grab a seat and I'll take care of it."

Cam returned minutes later and unloaded their tray.

Jill bit into the warm scone and moaned. "Lovely. How did you find this place? No offense, but it doesn't seem at all like you."

"My mother actually. And talk about not fitting. I thought she was kidding when she told me I should come here."

"Well, sometimes mothers can surprise us."

He sprinkled sugar into his latte and stirred.

"I finished your article for LNO. Annie will be so pleased. It's positive and informative. You certainly captured what she's trying to accomplish. And I appreciate the fact that you didn't focus too much on me or my clothing line."

"That's sort of what I wanted to talk to you about." He set the spoon aside. "I'd like to do a story about you and your work with the teens and connect it with your earlier work with the homeless."

She took a sip of her coffee. "Doesn't sound worth telling if you ask me. I really haven't done that much."

"On the contrary. You've done more than most people."

"Thank you, but I've already had a story about me and the homeless." She rolled her eyes. "Well, not exactly a story, more like a long paragraph and frankly, I don't think I want any more publicity."

And that was exactly why he needed to tell her story. He wanted to undo what Eagle Eye had done. She needed some good press. The sooner he could write a positive article about Jillian Jeffrey of JJ Designs, the better he'd feel. He'd write it under his real name and the Eagle, be damned.

"I also think it's a chance for you to let the world know about Steve. Tell his story and in doing so maybe help others like him. If we could paint an emotional picture about your work with Steve and what happened to him, I believe it would turn the hearts of many in the city and make them aware of the plight of the homeless."

Why hadn't he considered this before? In the past as the Eagle, he'd proudly pointed out the flaws of those in power. Always certain to make his point and entertain at the same time.

But did he actually help the needy in the process? There were so many good people, unknown heroes helping the poor. Like Spencer Keith and everyone who helped out at New Hope Soup Kitchen, then there was Margaret at the Bell Home for Orphan girls. And, of course, Jill. Jill who'd taught him, *honey is better than vinegar.*

He could and *should* be telling their stories.

"I tell you what." Jill broke off a piece of pastry and popped it between her lips. "I promise I'll think about it, okay?"

"Okay." Cam forked a generous piece of scone. "I know this is short notice. And that you'll probably have to make a dress for the occasion, but will you go with me to one of my boring Christmas parties on Friday night? There'll be dancing."

Jill's lips parted in a radiant smile. "I love to dance. And I'd be happy to go with you."

"It's a date, then."

CHAPTER TWENTY-ONE

Wow. Cam stood in the middle of Jill's foyer eyeing her with appreciation. "Jill, your dress is amazing." Taking her hand, he slowly twirled her around, briefly pausing when he saw her bare back. Not at all what she usually wore.

The dress fit Miss Jeffrey in all the right places and revealed others he'd never had the pleasure of seeing before. She was radiant, glowing, like all the magic and wonder of the holidays.

"You're stunning. You look like Christmas."

"Wait." She eyed him with an adorable frown. "Is that a compliment?"

"It is indeed." He smiled. "You're lovely."

"Thank you."

"What can I say, you bring out the *adult* in me."

"And to think I thought you were a teenager the first time I saw you."

"What?"

Oh no. That had been Phil. "Ah, yes, you remember…on the elevator."

"Right, on the elevator. When you refused to look at me."

"I did, didn't I? More fool me." He took her hand. "Are you ready?"

"Where are we off to?"

"It's a surprise."

Ten minutes later, the Plaza Hotel came into view.

"Out of all the swanky hotels in the city this one's my favorite," Jill said.

"Mine, too."

"Don't you just love the fairy tale atmosphere of the place? The history?"

"I do."

The party was in full swing when they entered the ballroom.

"The buffet line is forming," Cam said. "Shall we eat first?"

"Let's, I'm starved."

After filling their plates, they found a seat tucked into the corner near one of the gilded columns.

Cam watched her take a bite of one of the creamy seafood dishes. He loved watching her participate in the simplest activity. Everything about her mesmerized him. He thought of her every waking moment and orchestrated each day to somehow include her.

The band started playing the Van Morrison song, "Have I Told You Lately."

"Shall we dance?"

"I'd love to." She dabbed her mouth with a napkin, then took his hand.

Cam led her to the dance floor and took her into his arms.

"I love this song," she said.

"Me, too. The lead singer sounds a lot like Van Morrison."

"I've always loved his raspy voice," Jill said. "Very romantic."

"Very." Unable to take his eyes off her, he simply stared, drinking in every curve of her beautiful face.

Jill gazed at him, her dreamy eyes sweet with longing. At this moment she looked blissfully happy and his heart surged knowing he was the cause of it.

The tenderness and warmth in her expression wasn't completely unexpected, but it touched him deeply.

Jill tucked her head underneath his chin and closed her eyes. He held her like this for the duration of the song. Wanted to go on holding her, wanted to feel her nestled against him. When she stepped away he reluctantly released her.

"That was lovely. Thank you."

He trailed his finger along the side of her face. "*You're* lovely."

She licked her lips and continued to gaze at him. "I think our food is getting cold."

"Right."

He placed his hand to her bare back and escorted her to their table, fingers tingling from her warm flesh.

For days he'd been trying to figure out a way to reveal his identity. As the Eagle and as Phil. He'd decided to start with Phil. At least she liked *him*. From there he'd figure a way to tell her he was Eagle Eye. But, first things, first.

When he'd received the invite to this particular party he thought it might be the answer he was looking for. Their unusual relationship started here and what better place than the Plaza Hotel for the big reveal.

He needed to pick the right moment, though. They'd eat, dance and enjoy some small talk. He'd let her know he had feelings for her, and depending on her response, tell her then. But as the evening progressed the right opportunity didn't present itself. Between the untimely interruptions from this friends and Jill's desire to dance every other number, he wondered if he'd ever have the chance.

After they finished dessert, Jill wanted to dance, again. As he walked her back to the floor, he took the moment to admire her. He'd told her she was lovely, but tonight she was a knockout. Especially in that dress. His gaze roamed to her spiked heels, which did all manner of *lovely* things to her legs. How a woman even danced in such shoes frankly amazed him.

Speaking of spiked heels - a tall, redhead approached them.

"Hello, Jill."

"Stephanie, hi. Cameron, this is Stephanie Avery. She's also in fashion. Stephanie, Cameron Phillips."

The two shook hands and Stephanie eyed him appreciatively, then turned her attention to Jill.

"I hear you're one of three designers up for LNO's board."

"Yes, I am."

If it were possible, Jill's smile became even more radiant.

"I would congratulate you," Stephanie continued, "but according to the article there are some who think using the homeless to raise the money, although clever and industrious of you, is still a bit underhanded. Or, don't you agree?"

Cam's heart stopped.

All the sparkle left Jill's face. Her glowing youthful happiness faded on the spot. "I— What article?"

"Were you aware I'm one of the designer's in play for LNO's board?"

Jill shook her head. "I hadn't heard. What article?"

"In the *Times*."

"The *Times*?"

Stephanie nodded. "Dan Carlyle's article. In spite of that, I do wish you good luck." She glanced beyond Jill. "Looks like I'm being summoned. Nice meeting you, Cameron."

Stephanie slinked off, blending within the crowd seconds later.

Cam's gut churned. What the hell just happened? What *Times'* article? He brushed his hand through his hair.

Jill stood motionless, then hastily made her way to their table. He followed, careful to keep some distance and to give Jill the privacy she sought.

She pulled her phone from her purse and quickly typed something on the screen. She stood, rigid and unmoving.

From his proximity, he was able to see the changing expressions on her face. She was openly distressed.

Cam, helpless to do anything at this point, closed the gap between them.

Wide-eyed and ghost-like, she turned to him. "I'm sorry. But, I have to leave."

This could not be happening. Not here. Not now. "Tell me what's wrong?" he said.

"An article from weeks ago. It's resurfaced." Her voice broke slightly. "I thought it was behind me. Apparently, it's been linked to another piece in today's *Times*." She shook her head, her face devoid of all color. "Will this ever end?"

Even though her voice had lowered to a whisper, every anguished word hit him between the eyes. Guilt overwhelmed him.

"Running away will only make it look worse, you know. It will only make them talk more."

Hesitant, she raised anxious-filled eyes to his. "Make what look worse? You know about it?"

"Nor will being in denial help."

The raw anguish on her face cut deep, which was no more than he deserved.

"What are you trying to say?"

"The article. What it says. About you." He held his breath. Any second now...

"How? How could—" Her jaw dropped.

She merely stared, tongue-tied. He watched the initial shock in her wide-eyed expression turn to utter pain. Watched as her imploring gaze searched his face for an answer and shaking her head as if that one act of physical denial could make it untrue.

"You're him. Aren't you?"

He'd hoped this moment would never come. Had hoped his article hadn't affected her. Who on earth was Dan Carlyle? Not that it mattered one whit at this point. This was not how he'd wanted her to find out.

In that moment, the entire room melted away. The laughter and festive holiday sounds fading into the background, until all he heard was her shallow, anxious breaths as she waited for his answer. But he just stood there. Mute. Until her questioning, hopeful 'none of this could be true' expression turned to one of helpless resignation.

A tremulous smile feathered across her mouth. "All this time, I had no idea. I've been fraternizing with the enemy." A low, anguished, half-chuckle escaped her lips. "So you could what? Gather more entertaining information about the user of the down-and-out?"

He lifted his hands. "Jill, listen—"

"Why me?"

The misery in her eyes cut him to the core.

"Did you just pick me out of a crowd and say, 'There's a naïve fool. I'll ruin her life.'"

"No. That's not what happened." He gripped her shoulders. "Let's go someplace where we can talk."

She clutched the pendant at her neck and glanced helplessly around the festive ballroom. "I've been a fool, thinking I could fit in."

"I was planning to tell you tonight. Here. At the Plaza." He ran his hand across the back of his neck.

But she wasn't hearing him. With hands gripped against her stomach, she gazed frantically around the room, as if looking for a way of escape. Tears welled in her eyes, but she bravely blinked them away. "I think it's time for me to go."

Without a backward glance, she turned and wove her petite frame through the crowded ballroom, past the gilt columns and crystal-laden tables. He, the great Eagle Eye, stared after her. The smug, know-it-all investigative reporter.

Speechless.

Guilty.

As she skirted the tables, not one person spoke to her or even acknowledged her departure. For these people the merriment of the season had gone undisturbed. Not so much for her.

He gazed around the ballroom, a bitter taste in his mouth. It seemed his noble quest to inform the public about certain issues had backfired. Until recently, he hadn't put much thought as to how his articles could be damaging someone's life or career.

The Eagle Eye had accused Jill of using a homeless man for her gain. But he'd done the same thing. Allowed his own blindness toward a certain group of people to cloud his usual, rational judgment.

Until this article, he'd always interviewed multiple sources and did his best to present all sides of an issue. But in this case he'd used only one source. Himself. He'd gone against every principle he'd sworn to uphold as a journalist and used *her* to make a point. How were his actions any different than what he'd accused her of doing?

No, Jill. You're not the fool. I am. He left the hotel, haunted by the pain and misery in her eyes.

CHAPTER TWENTY-TWO

Cam stuffed chopsticks with the last bit of the cashew chicken between his lips, then tossed the square to-go box from Chen Wong's in the trash. It had taken all of his emotional energy to set aside his concern for Jill and finish his latest article.

Shifting mental gears had never been this much work. In the middle of a paragraph, the door chimed. He clicked *save* and closed his laptop.

He crossed the low-pile area rug, then yanked open the door. Caught off guard at the sight of the well-dressed older woman standing in his doorway, he sucked in a breath.

"Hello, Mother." He held the door while she stepped inside, then kissed her on the cheek. "I haven't seen you in ages."

"And whose fault is that?"

"Mine, of course."

She held a folded newspaper to his face. "What is this?"

"A...newspaper?"

"And when did you write it?"

Cam rued the day he'd ever told his mother he was the Eagle Eye.

"Weeks ago. And if you ever read anything other than the *Times*, you would've known about it."

"True, but I hate the way you expose people's motives. What if someone did that to me?"

"Then I would most certainly come to your defense."

"You attacked a fashion designer?" She slapped the paper on his side table.

"I didn't *attack* her." He already felt terrible about it without his mother ragging him. And if she knew the full story, she'd be more than angry. She'd be disappointed in him and it would be deserved.

He stepped aside, allowing her to enter his living area ahead of him.

"Not only a designer," she continued, "but a teen girl one?" Exasperated, she plopped into the nearest chair.

He took a seat across from hers. "Then next time, I'll be sure to get your permission as to who I can and cannot write about." Trying to make light of the situation only made him feel worse.

"Don't mock me. This is my industry."

"No. It is *not* your industry. It's just another one of your entrepreneurial *dabblings*."

"I do not dabble. Besides, you won't take the money so I might as well invest it for you. You may be young now, but you'll retire some day."

He bit back a smile. "Thank you, Mother."

"But a teen girl designer? Seriously? This is not a laughing matter."

"And I'm not laughing. But you're acting like I've criticized a helpless, teenage girl instead of a twenty-five-year-old adult woman."

"Criticized? Is that what you call it?" Cam's mother crossed her arms and glared at him.

He ran both hands through his hair and huffed a sigh. "As a journalist, I have a job to do. And I take it seriously. Now if you'll excuse me, I have a deadline."

She stood, placed one hand on her hip, then cast a shrewd glance over his place.

Still seated, he folded his arms and stared at her. "What is it?"

"How can you stand living in such cramped quarters when we have a house in Scarsdale and the Hamptons?"

He stood, placed a hand under her elbow and escorted his mother out of the room. "Convenience, for one."

When they reached the front door, he took hold of his mother's upper arms and turned her toward him. "And two. I like my small New York loft apartment." He lowered his head and kissed her cheek. "Now, I love you and I promise never to let this much time go by between our visits."

She sighed heavily. "I love you, too." She shoved the news article against his chest. "Please make this right."

As she left the apartment, he heard her mumble something about him being just like his father.

* * *

Cam arrived at the Hollisters' Christmas party fashionably late. Solid lead or not, after what happened with Jill, he was in no mood to party. He'd avoided this type of gathering for several years, but couldn't very well refuse Beverly's invitation.

The butler escorted him to a grand living room glittering with Christmas decorations. Ladies in festive evening gowns, diamond necklaces, and men in black rounded out the opulent setting. Minutes later, he spotted Beverly Blake across the room. She caught his eye and motioned for him to come over.

"You dress up nicely. That tux looks custom."

"It is."

"Snob," she chuckled. "Cameron, this is David Cummings. The gentleman I told you about. David, Cameron."

Cameron shook David's hand. "Nice to meet you."

"Likewise. I understand you need information for a story on the possible merger of AT&T and Time Warner."

"I do. Beverly told me you're in the city. Is there a time next week we could meet?"

"Absolutely."

Both men opened the calendar app on their phones.

"How does Wednesday morning at nine o'clock sound?" David said.

"Sounds great. I look forward to it."

Beverly took Cam's arm and led him across the room. "That worked out nicely."

"It did, thanks."

"Since when are you interested in mergers?"

'I'm not. But freelance journalists can't always be particular about their subject matter." He shrugged. "This article will pay my electric bill for three months. It's that simple."

"You're the only single male I know who's as wealthy as sin, but refuses to live off his mother's millions."

"Not interested."

"Too many strings?"

"Exactly."

At that moment a tall middle-aged man entering the ballroom caught Beverly's eye.

"That's Darrin Bishop. I need to speak with him before someone else grabs his attention." She patted Cam's arm. "Let's talk later."

"Okay."

A waitress walked by with a tray filled with sparkling wine. She paused briefly in front of Cam and smiled. "Wine, sir?"

Cam lifted the long-stemmed glass from the silver tray. He took a sip and glanced around the festive ballroom. Silver and gold ornaments clustered in mass amongst the greenery threading the enormous staircase. Matching décor scrolled across the stone mantel on the fireplace at the far the end of the room. At the beginning of the season, the *Post* had done an expose on the Hollisters' home. It was even more beautiful in person. He so wished Jill were here with him. She would have loved the festive décor.

He sipped his wine and watched Beverly laugh at something Darrin Bishop had said. Beverly could work a room like no one else. As former city editor of the *Post*, her contacts were many. The Week End News was lucky to have her. As one of his best resources, she could be depended on for the introduction to David Cummings or anyone else he might need in the future.

He gazed around the gilded, ornate room and wondered how he'd escaped the social scene for as long as he had. He'd grown up with it. Born into wealth, his life had been easy. After college he'd gone to Haiti to work with The Water Project. When he came back home, adjusting to wealth and position had been a challenge. He would never see the world the same way again.

Even with that, he'd learned to keep a balance. By no means was he going to leave it all and live in some commune. He was thankful for his family and his heritage, but knew he could never fully go back to his playboy party days. He'd use his gifts and his wealth to help those less fortunate. Much as he'd tried to continue with the lavish parties, over time he'd grown more and more uninterested.

Unfortunately, his mother didn't see it that way. To please her, he'd managed to make one or two major social events each year. His mother would be beside herself when she discovered he'd been to the Hollisters' Christmas party. It was renowned for one of Scarsdale's best social events of the season.

A middle-aged gentleman sauntered up and stood beside him.

"Quite a gathering, isn't it?" he said.

"I was just thinking the same thing."

The man held out his right hand. "Nicolas Jeffrey. I live a few blocks from the Hollisters."

For a millisecond Cam froze. *Nicolas Jeffrey.* Pulling himself together, he stuck out his hand. "Cameron Phillips, nice to meet you."

"Scarsdale's social scene is fairly small. I haven't seen you since I moved back. Are you new to the area?"

"I spent my childhood here, but grew up in the city. My grandfather still lives here. He started the Phillips Law Firm."

"That's on Overhill Road isn't it?"

"Yes. He's no longer there of course. He retired years ago."

"So what line of work are you in?"

"I'm a journalist. Formally with the *New York Post* and am now freelance."

"Married? Family?"

Cam smiled. "Still single."

Nicolas nodded to two beautifully dressed young women across the room. They were holding champagne glasses and talking to what looked to be their dates. "My daughters. I keep hoping one of them will get married and give my wife and me grandchildren."

A few days ago he'd have assumed this man to be Jill's father. He could see the headline now—Cam Phillips makes a fool of himself.

Nicolas eyed him with a glint of humor. "Something on your mind, son?"

"Oh, uh. I'm just a bit embarrassed. Until a few days ago, I'd confused your family with another family named Jeffrey. With a particular young woman, actually. Twenty-five, about so high." He lifted his hand to chest height. "Goes by the name of Jill?"

He believed Jill but the journalist in him just had to make sure.

Nicolas shook his head. "As you can see, my girls are a bit taller than that. And none of them are named Jill."

"I realize that now. Forgive me for being blunt, but considering your notoriety there are very few photos of your daughters online."

"You've been researching my daughters?"

"Oh, no. My research had to do with the other Jeffrey. The girl I just mentioned. And your daughters did come up. Even without photos, speculation and gossip about your family are too tempting for some columnists to ignore."

"My advice, don't believe even half of what you hear."

Cam nodded. "I am curious, though. How have they escaped being photographed?"

"Body guards." A shrewd twinkle appeared in Jeffrey's eye. "I'm a very wealthy man."

Well, at least that part was true.

Someone hailed Nicolas from across the room. "If you'll excuse me."

"Of course." Cam sipped his drink, his mind swirling in a million directions.

Throughout the rest of the evening, he thought of little else but making things right with Jill. As he stood brooding, a familiar voice spoke behind him.

"Cameron. What a nice surprise."

Of course. That's it. She was his answer.

He turned and gave the older woman a hug. "Hello, Mother. You're just the person I wanted to see."

CHAPTER TWENTY-THREE

Jill stood before the door of her childhood home and knocked.

"Jill." Mary Jeffrey hugged her daughter. "Why didn't you tell us you were coming home? We weren't expecting you until Christmas."

Jill stepped through the door, pulling her suitcase behind her.

"How long can you stay?"

"A long time."

"Honey, what happened?"

Jill burst into tears.

"Oh, sweetie." Mary enveloped Jill, then with her arm over her shoulders, led her toward the living room. "Come sit down. I'll fix us a cup of tea, then you can tell me all about it."

Jill took a seat on the sofa while her mom went to the kitchen. A few minutes later, Mary returned with two cups of Darjeeling. "Here you go. Sweet, just the way you like it."

"Thanks." Jill cradled the china in her hands, then gave her mom the short version leading up to her departure. Beginning at the fundraiser, she told her mom everything. Except for the identity of the Eagle Eye. That was still raw and much too painful to talk about.

Mary wrapped her arms around Jill and held her. "Honey, I'm so sorry. I know how badly this must have hurt you." She pulled away and looked her in the eye. "But I wouldn't give up on your dream. You're young and you have a rare gift with fabrics and color and design. New York is not the end-all you know."

Jill forced a smile for her mother's benefit. Her mom meant well, but right now it looked more like the end, than a beginning. "Thanks, Mom."

In silence they went back to their tea. "Did you actually close the workroom?" Mary asked.

Jill stared into her cup and sighed. "Not yet. The others don't know I've decided to pack it in, but I'm sure Amy's figured it out by now. Frankly, she could see it coming even before I did. I'll tell them after Christmas. I've ruined everything else. Why ruin the holidays if I don't have to."

"Don't say that. You haven't ruined anything."

"Spoken like a true mom."

"Give it some time, honey. People forget."

"And who knows," Jill said, "maybe after the holidays there'll be another scandalous news story to talk about."

"Honey, no one who knows you would ever put *you* and *scandalous* in the same sentence."

"Well, unfortunately for me, not everyone in New York knows me. But now, thanks to the Eagle Eye and this Dan person, they think they do." She placed the cup on the coffee table. "Between articles and Mark, Phil, a sweet old lady and Cameron thinking I'm a Jeffrey of Scarsdale, I've had it with these people."

"A who?"

"Jeffrey of Scarsdale. Three sisters who, from everything I've heard, think the world rotates solely around them. But who knows, I've been maligned, so maybe they've been, too." She stood up. "I'm going out for a while."

"Are you sure? I mean—"

"Mom. I'm not suicidal. I'm going to the lighthouse. It always worked for Katie. Maybe I'll find an answer there."

* * *

Jill approached the curve in the road giving her the first full view of Paige Point Light. *Katie's light* as she'd often thought of it. She wondered about her dearest friend and decided to make the drive to the Keeper's House.

The white clapboard structure and the small matching cottage had been completely renovated five years earlier and beautifully restored by Katie's husband, Max Sawyer.

When she pulled her car up in front of the main house she could tell no one was home. Katie and Max were probably at one of their other properties. As a hotel developer, Max specialized in exclusive boutique hotels. Several of which were light stations. He and Katie had kept this one as a private residence.

With only her scarf to keep warm, Jill got out and bolted for the tower. Happy to find the heavy metal door unlocked, she trudged her way to the top. The candle room gave a breathtaking view of the wintery waters of the Chesapeake Bay. She gazed out over the wide expanse. Beauty and mystery wove its own magical spell to whoever dared to look.

Her friend Katie had a special love affair with the lighthouse and the surrounding compound. Standing here now, looking out over the bay, Jill could certainly understand why. A place to dream big dreams, or in her case, to bring one's sorrows—it was always there.

Jill tugged her scarf into a knot at her neck, then blew her warm breath into her hands. She wondered how many whispered prayers had been sent out from this place of solitude.

"Who goes there?"

Jill spun at the deep, gravelly voice. "Pop!"

A wide grin formed on Angus MacAfee's rugged face. Katie's grandfather stood tall and spry just inside the candle room.

Jill gave the elderly man a fierce hug, which he reciprocated with more strength than one would expect from his frail body. "I hope it's okay that I'm up here?"

"Of course. Where's your coat?"

"I left it at the house. You look wonderful, Pop. Did you and Bessie discover the fountain of youth since I last saw you?"

"My Bessie is the reason." He winked. "Marrying a younger woman has kept me spry."

Jill couldn't help but smile. Bessie was at least seventy and she and Pop had been married for about five years now.

"And how is Bessie?"

"Still round and sassy, and I wouldn't change a thing." Pop chuckled. "You just missed Max and Katie. They left two days ago for California."

"Sorry I missed them."

"But you didn't come to see them."

She shook her head.

"What brings you to our lighthouse, then?"

Jill shrugged. "I just needed some time away from the big city."

"Well, that lost puppy dog look in your eyes better not have been put there by some scoundrel."

She groaned. "It was actually, but not in the way you're thinking."

"What other way is there?"

"This man wrote an article and mentioned me in the not-so-nice part."

Angus shook his head. "Uppity city folk. Pay them no mind."

"They're not all like him. I've met some wonderful people in New York."

"If it's so great, then why come back here?"

"Oh, Pop, you don't mince words do you?"

"Life's too short not to say what you mean. Besides, I've never known you to run away from a fight or a mean newspaper article. It's only words on a page, darlin'."

"I guess I am running away." She sighed. "I just wanted to feel safe. At least here, I know people love me."

"What's not to love? We've all seen you grow up. And a fine young lass you've become, too."

During her college years, Angus MacAfee had been a stand-in grandfather to her on more than one occasion. His constant blue-eyed twinkle held both wisdom and warmth. As Paige Point, Maryland's last keeper of the light, he was beloved by everyone in the sleepy fishing village and in all of the Chesapeake Bay area. Jill wrapped her arms around Angus. "Thanks, Pop. You're just what the doctor ordered."

"Ach, doctors. Take no mind to them, either."

* * *

Cameron flagged the nearest taxi, barked out Jill's address, sat back and waited for the inevitable. He hoped to God it wasn't too late. He had a lot to explain and didn't want to waste another minute.

He mounted the steps to Jill's brownstone and pressed the doorbell. He glanced at his watch. Eleven thirty. He wondered where she could be at this hour. Although it was highly likely she was ignoring him. He certainly hoped she hadn't gone to the tent city. Concerned for her safety, he flagged a taxi and went there himself.

He entered the subway and made his way to Eddie's spot. "Eddie, wake up."

A long minute later, Eddie poked his head out of the tent. "We don't usually see the likes of you down here," he said.

"Eddie, it's me, Phil."

The look on Eddie's face would have been comical if Cam hadn't been concerned about Jill's whereabouts.

Eddie gave him a highly skeptical once-over, then grinned. "It *is* you. You win the lottery?"

"No." He smiled. "Listen, I'm looking for a young woman."

"Aren't we all?"

Cam laughed. "Do you remember the petite young woman that came looking for me?"

"The one I saw you with the last time you were here?"

"That's the one."

Eddie shook his head. "Haven't seen her. You two an item?"

He shoved his hands into his pockets. "I screwed up."

Eddie rubbed his frayed, gloved hand across his stubble. "Sorry to hear, man."

"Look, buddy. I need to run. Do you need anything? Is there something I can bring you?"

"I need a whole lot of things, but right now you'd better keep after that girl."

"I plan to. Thanks. Nice tent, by the way," Cam said. "And I see you have enough propane to get you through the winter."

"And how would you know?" Eddie's eyes held a twinkle that said he already knew the answer.

Cam hadn't taken two steps before Eddie called out to him.

"Hold up." Eddie ducked into his tent. After twenty seconds of rummaging and tossing items from inside the tent, Cam flicked back his cuff to check the time. "Eddie, what the—"

"Got it!" Eddie reappeared clutching the cashmere coat. "I saved this for you. Figured no man in his right mind would want to part with it."

An image of Jill dressed in hot pink, handing him the coat, filled his mind's eye. The sudden, overwhelming ache in his heart could not be denied. He loved Jill Jeffrey. And wanted to spend a lifetime getting to know her.

"Thanks." They shook hands. "By the way, what happened with the interview I set up for you?"

"I start in January."

Cam smiled. "Merry Christmas, Eddie."

Clutching the cashmere to his chest, Cam flagged the next taxi he saw and headed for his apartment. He still had no idea where Jill was. Hopefully she was with one of her friends. He'd broken her heart and had no idea if she'd even talk with him, but he had to try.

* * *

Monday morning Cam arrived at JJ Designs to find the place practically empty. Amy was just opening up.

"Morning, Amy. Jill here yet?"

"Nope." He followed Amy through the offices while she flicked on the lights. It wasn't like Amy to ignore him. She was usually chatty, offering him coffee and muffins.

"When do you expect her?"

"Not sure."

Amy's abrupt attitude further intrigued him. He stuffed his hands into his pockets and followed her. "With fashion week just around the corner, I'm surprised she's not already here."

Amy grunted and continued down the hallway to the kitchen.

"She and I were getting together this morning." When Amy didn't respond he said, "Is everything all right?"

Amy paused, glanced back at him, then flicked on the kitchen lights. "It's not for me to say."

"I've texted Jill a few times, but she's not responding," he said. "Have you talked to her this morning? Has she left you any messages?"

"No."

"I went by her place last night and she wasn't home."

"I know."

Cameron placed his hand on Amy's arm stopping her mid-stride. "Hey, I can tell when something's wrong."

Amy sighed and gazed up at him. "She'll probably kill me. But after the past couple of days I don't know how telling you could make things any worse."

"What things? What happened?"

"This whole mess started with that blasted Eagle person."

He cringed at the scathing drip in Amy's voice. "What?"

"That Eagle Eye article on the homeless. You must know about it. You're in the business."

"Oh. Yeah. Him."

"Maybe you haven't read it. Probably not your kind of thing. You're way too nice."

Cam tugged at his shirt collar. Actually, he hadn't been nice. Far from it. Guilt rose by the second as he stood listening to Amy. At least he still had a conscience. That was something.

"How did the article affect Jill?" He pretty much knew the answer, but had to ask.

"This 'bottom dweller' put Jill in a terrible light about something she did at a fundraiser last month. The good news, he never actually mentioned her name so the original article didn't seem to hurt us much." Amy frowned, clearly disgusted with the situation.

She stepped to the coffee maker and added water. "We were sick about it, but what could we do? Nada. We were both on pins and needles the week the article came out. And except for one small cancellation, no one else seemed to notice. We breathed a sigh and went about our work." Amy grabbed a clean mug and poured. "Coffee?"

"No thanks."

"Anyway, two weeks ago we got a huge break. Sloan's fell in love with Jill's latest fall line, and placed a substantial order for their back-to-school section. Exclusive to Sloan's. That's a big deal in case you don't know. The buyer left and verbally promised to place their order the following week. We took that as a done deal and because of the time crunch, we ordered everything. The fabric, the notions, the accessories."

"School is months away. Why order so early?"

"Back-to-school clothes are in stores as early as July. That only gave us six months to design the line, have it approved, and have everything made and ready to ship to Sloan's warehouse." Amy spread her hands in a hopeless gesture. "This order was the *dream* order, the culmination of everything Jill's worked for. Then two days ago, the buyer called and informed us they would not be making the order after all."

"That's disappointing."

"Understatement. Anyway, two days ago, Eagle Eye's article was linked to another piece in the *Times*. Sloan's buyer got wind of it. And if Sloan's knows about it, then so does everyone else."

"Oh."

"*Oh no,* is more like it. JJ Designs is now broke. If we don't get another buyer soon, JJ Designs is through. And I have to tell you, that's a slim option at best."

He'd done this. Sabotaged everything Jill had worked for. "Have you tried to reach her?"

"Of course. I've called, texted and emailed, but the only response I get is a text telling all of us here to take a few days off and go Christmas shopping. She said she'd keep me posted on when she's planning to return, and that was two days ago. But, that's not all. I can tell something else has happened besides the cancellation."

God help him, he was that something else. "Did she mention what it was?"

"No. But I could tell by the sound of her voice it was bad. I don't think it was about the business either as I'm privy to that side of things. This was personal. She was clearly upset."

"Do you mind telling me where she went? Maybe there's something I can do."

"She went home."

"I checked again this morning. She's either not there or not answering."

"No. Home to Paige Point."

"Paige Point?"

"Maryland. It's a fishing village on the Chesapeake Bay, near St. Michaels."

"That's right. I remember now. Thanks."

After he left the building, he sprinted across the street and hailed a cab. He had no idea where Paige Point was located. But after rescheduling his meeting with David Cummings, he caught an afternoon flight from New York to Easton, Maryland.

After he arrived, he grabbed a map at the Hertz counter, then drove the short thirteen miles into Paige Point. It was getting dark by the time he arrived. The cold little town shivered on the edge of the Chesapeake Bay. It was empty and almost ghost-like.

Instead of stopping to eat, he followed Amy's directions to the Jeffrey home. He pulled up in front of a simple two-story yellow house and stopped. It was one of several nestled beside a picturesque marina. A variety of small boats were safely moored along the weathered dock adjacent to the houses.

As he walked up the narrow stone pathway, he tried Jill's cell, but again, no answer. The red paint on the front door had faded over time and had worn off completely near the knob. While he stood assessing the condition of the paint he realized how awkward this could get. He blew out a breath, fisted his hand and knocked.

A stocky, nice looking, middle-aged man, opened the door.

"May I help you?"

"Hi, yes. My name is Cameron Phillips. I'm a friend of Jill's from New York. Her co-worker Amy Stallings said I might find her here."

"I'm sorry, Jill's gone back to New York. Come on in. I'm Miles, her dad."

Cameron stepped through the door and was met with the most amazing aroma, which did all manner of wonderful things to his mid-section. Something similar to his grandmother's Sunday pot roast drifted from the kitchen. He hadn't eaten since breakfast, and his stomach rumbled traitorously. Miles led him to the living room.

"So, she's already gone back?" This just wasn't his day.

"I'm afraid so. She has to attend a function, tomorrow evening... For some charity she volunteers for."

"Like No Other?"

"That's the one."

"I'm actually planning to be there, as well."

A trim woman and a teenage boy appeared from another room.

"Honey, this is Cameron Phillips. He's a friend of Jill's from New York."

"Cameron, this is my wife, Mary, and our son, Jamey."

"Hi. It's so nice to meet you." Mary placed her slender hand in his.

"Nice to meet you, Mary," Cameron said. "I hope I'm not intruding." He noticed the teenage boy was the same young man who was with Jill in the city several weeks ago.

"Hey." Jamey thrust out his hand and clasped Cam's firmly.

"Hi, Jamey. You must be Jill's brother." Jamey beamed a grin as the two shook hands. Hit with the humor of the situation, Cam smiled. It was all coming clear.

"Cameron, we were just about to sit down to dinner," Mary said. "If you haven't already eaten, we'd love for you to join us."

Cameron slapped his palm against his stomach. "I thought you'd never ask."

CHAPTER TWENTY-FOUR

Jill sat at the table waiting for her turn at the podium, having barely touched her meal. Her stomach churned with debilitating nerves. The dinner guests consisted of who's who in the fashion world and even some in the media. All present to celebrate the third anniversary of Like No Other.

Cameron was supposed to be in attendance as well, but so far she hadn't seen him. Apparently his LNO article had come out in this morning's addition of the *Post*. Annie had been more than pleased with it, attributing LNO's sudden turnaround to Cam's positive article. And from the looks of the guest list, things had most certainly turned a corner for her and the foundation.

Annie touched Jill's hand. "Everything's going to be fine."

"I appreciate your confidence, but I fear it may be misplaced in my instance."

"I of all people know how unfair some in the media can be. And the board agrees. I know your heart, Jill, and I want you on my team."

Jill smiled and nodded, but even Annie's assurances wouldn't deter Jill from doing what she had to do.

She gazed out at the sea of faces sitting at white cloth-covered tables, sipping the after-dinner coffee provided by the hotel. At this point, most if not *all* probably knew she was the one referred to by Eagle Eye. And most likely believed she didn't deserve the award she was here to receive. Her heart had been in the right place, her motives pure, but right now she had to admit, she agreed with them. She could not accept this award in light of what everyone in her industry believed to be true. The next ten minutes would be excruciating, but she was determined to get through it.

As she sat pondering her predicament, she spotted Cameron entering the ballroom at the back. The Eagle had arrived. It was only appropriate he should be here to witness the final blow to her career.

She barely heard Anna Delany's glowing introduction. Would Annie despise her after this? With the Alex Langdon situation finally resolved, would her presence and this evening's event add fuel to a fire so recently put out?

The apathetic applause pulled Jill out of her reverie. She drew in a deep breath, then slowly let it out, stood and stepped up to the podium.

"Thank you for your kind words, Anna." She forced the appropriate smile, gripping the sides of the dais for support. "Twenty thousand dollars is indeed a wonderful contribution of which I can take little credit. I was fortunate to help raise the money and for that I'm thankful. I know the funds will go to good use in this fine organization."

She licked her dry lips and continued. "I want to tell you a story about a man who lives between a bridge and an abandoned subway station. Even though he is homeless and lost, he is no less a man." She swallowed and took a steadying breath. "Since when does someone's circumstances dictate the worth of the person? No one has the right to use someone because they have nothing. There is no honor in that, no matter how good the cause.

"This man is not alone in how he lives. There are many others like him. At one time every one of these unfortunate people was

204 · DARCY FLYNN

someone's child, dearly loved by a mom or a dad. What happened to transform them from an adored toddler to becoming a lost teenager or adult, who now wanders the city looking for food and a warm place to sleep at night? I'm neither a social worker nor a psychologist, so I'm not here to answer those questions. But to say this…

"By now, many of you have read the article by Eagle Eye. The piece refers to a young female up-and-coming teen fashion designer who used a homeless man for financial gain. That is only partially true. The financial gain was not for herself, but for a charity foundation. *This* foundation." She licked her lips. "For those of you wondering or simply too polite to ask, yes, that designer is me.

"The article states the money came through deception. I can honestly say that is *not* true. Let me assure you, the check I've recently donated was not acquired under false pretenses, as the article states. And even though my motives were good, the article is correct when it says my method was not.

"Oh, I rationalized. Told myself I was doing a good deed. After all, what could be so wrong with giving a homeless man a warm coat and a hot meal in a beautiful hotel ballroom? You see, in the process of obtaining that amount, I hurt that homeless man. Not physically, but I caused him pain just the same."

She paused and gazed over the audience. "For the past two years, I've admired the work of Anna Delany and Like No Other." She dipped her head to the teenage guests sitting down front. "I've always wanted to find a way to use my talent in fashion to help others. And then I discovered Like No Other." She glanced briefly at Annie. Alarm flowed from her friend's expressive eyes. "I so wanted to be a part of this organization.

"The lives of these young women sitting here on the front row have been influenced by Annie's fun and informative workshops, and her practical life principles, which go far beyond the teenage years. I'm truly thankful to have been a small part of that. Being here with all of you on this special night has been one of the highlights of my life. This organization is top notch, above suspicion, and exemplary in every way.

"Because my former actions have brought suspicion to this fine organization, it is with much personal regret that I cannot accept this award or your generous offer to be on your board."

She sucked in a deep breath, blinking back the threatening tears. "As a result of the Eagle Eye piece, I am no longer in a position to help with fundraising. My actions gave the appearance of selfishness, ruthless ambition, and insensitivity. Not to this organization, but to that man. I insulted him and for that I'm truly sorry. I publicly apologize to him, wherever he is."

She gazed out over the crowded room. Their judgment had turned to pity. In that moment she knew her career had ended. Her throat closed up. There was nothing else to say. She left the podium and walked off the stage.

* * *

Cameron quickly left the event, crossed the carpeted hallway, and exited through a side door. Hoping to catch up with Jill, he made his way to the front entrance, but she wasn't there. Then he spotted her. She was already across the street entering a cab. He hailed one on the corner and gave instructions to follow behind. From the route of the cab up ahead, Jill was heading to her office.

Fifteen minutes later, he stood at the entrance to JJ Designs and knocked. He could tell the lights inside were off because the usual glow from behind the frosted glass wasn't there. He couldn't stand the thought of her sitting alone in the dark.

"Jill! Open up. It's Cam."

No response.

Nothing.

He ran his hand around the back of his neck, grabbed the door handle and turned. It was unlocked.

He stepped inside the semi-darkness and glanced around. Light from the street seeped through the wall of venetian blinds on the opposite end of the room. Dust motes drifted through the air.

Feeling a bit like a thief, he slowly made his way across the floor to Jill's office. Not wanting to startle her, again he called out.

"Jill. It's Cam."

He stopped mid-stride when he saw her. A single lamp glowed from one corner of her work area. Her face and eyes were puffy from crying. Still wearing the pale pink sleeveless dress from earlier, she sat resting her left cheek against her fist while fingering the edge of fabric with her other hand.

"Pretty fabric," he said.

Jill slowly lifted her head, gave him a brief glance, then refocused on the cloth.

"It's a tartan plaid." She ran her hand along the bolt. "Very pretty. Sloan's thought so, too. It was supposed to become a jumper for fifth and sixth grade girls. It's the last chance for them to be little girls." Her lips tugged into a wistful smile.

"Amy told me they'd cancelled. Seems rather fast. I mean, the article just came out."

She lifted a delicate shoulder. "You know how it is. People talk. Word gets around." She continued to finger the cloth.

"Jill, I'm sorry."

"How can I help you, Cameron?"

He gripped the back of the vacant chair. "I came by to see if you were all right."

A low chuckle escaped her lips. "I'm great. The biggest order of my life has been cancelled. My business is bankrupt. And I'm the fool of my industry."

"This is my fault."

"Aww, that's so sweet. But, it's a bit late to go all gallant and noble, don't you think? Besides, I have to take some of the responsibility for the mess I'm in." She pressed her hands to her heart. "I'm as angry at me as I am with you. I tried to compete in a world in which I obviously don't belong."

She gazed up at him, hands still on her heart as if pleading for him to understand.

Her dejected body cried, yet she didn't shed a single tear.

"Don't say that."

"Tell me. Am I the only one who *knows* who you are?" Her voice broke.

"There are four now, counting you."

A light of revelation appeared in her eyes. "I see why you're here. You're worried I'll reveal your secret identity."

"No, that's not—"

"So." She rocked back in her chair. "This is what it's like to have leverage over someone. I rather like this feeling. Especially since it's directed at you. Tell me. Is this how you feel after one of your vile articles?" She practically spat at him.

He chewed his inner lip and watched her.

"What? You thought you were the only one who could wield cutting words like a double-edged sword? Rest easy, Eagle. Your secret is safe with me." The loathing in her eyes sickened him.

He fisted his hands and brought them to his mouth. Silently watching her, knowing there wasn't a snarky, sarcastic, bone in her body.

"You know, it's too bad you've already finished the LNO article because these last few days would have fit in well. More fodder for your readers. Lending the final blow to my career."

"Jill—"

"After all, a bird of prey is *always* present at the death. I hear they like to pick that last bit of flesh off the bones."

He slowly blinked and lifted a hand. "Jill, listen—"

"Don't feel so bad. I'm sure there are a few small-town boutiques somewhere in the county that don't read the *Times* or the *Post*."

"About what you said tonight…"

She swiveled in her seat, pulled a plastic binder from the shelf, and placed it in front of her. "You know, for someone who's known for his way with words, you're not saying very much."

"You haven't given me much of a chance."

Jill shifted in her seat. Back ridged, she primly folded her hands. "Now, if you'll excuse me, I have some damage control to attend to."

"At midnight?" Cam stuffed his hands into his pockets.

Jill's eyes locked onto his face, unblinking and accusatory. "I'm sorry, did I ask for your opinion?"

"I don't blame you for hating me."

"And here I thought it was you who hated me." For one moment she'd dropped her guard and the raw pain in her eyes was about his undoing. For lack of anything better to do in that moment, he picked up the empty tumbler and sniffed.

"Now that's just funny," she said. "You actually think what you've done has led me to alcohol?"

She giggled, a broken sound that lacked its usual joy.

"This," she stood and ran her hand across her body, "is me *not* drinking. There are so many other good ways to drown one's sorrows. Shopping for one. And buddy after today I plan to do my share. That is after I find another job and start earning some money so I can pay all my bills."

Tossing her hair in defiance, she marched down the hall away from him.

He hustled after her. "If you'd just calm down and give me one second—"

They reached the break room and she spun toward him. "Why aren't you gone?"

He clenched his jaw. He'd done this. Caused this open, caring woman to build a spiteful wall. Well he had news for her, no way would he let her keep him out.

"Look, I know I've caused you pain, and you have every right to hate me, but I refuse to leave you like this."

"Hey!" She attacked like a feral kitten. "After what you've done? You've got some nerve trying to boss me. I want you out. *Now*."

"Jill, I promise. Somehow, I'm going to make this right."

"Somehow? Now there's a comforting word." She barked out a laugh. "I'm hopeful already."

She spun away. He grabbed her arm and turned her to face him.

Chest heaving, hands fisted, she railed at him. "What part of *I want you to leave*, don't you understand?"

She grabbed a spoon from the counter and threw. Cam flinched and ducked. He hunkered low against the onslaught. A barrage of assorted items came at him as Jill snatched up and tossed item after item through the air. As he straightened up, a pack of plastic coffee stirrers hit him in his chest. But when she made a grab for a large tin of coffee he panicked. He eyed the shower behind her. Hopes for a rational conversation had long gone, so he ducked down, placed his shoulder at her hip and lifted.

"What the— Put me down!"

Ignoring her protests, Cam carried her over his shoulder while systematically slipping off one high heel then the other.

"What are you doing?"

"Cooling you off."

As she dangled over his shoulder, he reached into the shower stall and turned on the water.

"No, don't. Stop! You don't understa—"

Cam planted her feet to the tile and held her underneath the flowing water.

Jill screeched and sputtered as the water poured over her head. With his arms banded around her, he held her there until they were both soaked to the skin. When her protests turned into sobs he turned off the water and held her against him.

He brushed wet hair from his forehead. "Hey. I'm sorry. But I didn't know how else to stop the rant."

She placed both hands against his chest and shoved. "You deplorable beast!" She grabbed the skirt part of her dress with both hands and shook. "I'm not crying because of that. This fabric is dry clean only," she wailed. "You've ruined it."

"Oh." He bit his lower lip, but his attempt to stifle his smile failed. "I'm sorry. I'll buy you a new one."

"It's not funny." She pushed her wet hair off her face. "For your information, this is a one-of-a-kind, JJ Design."

"Then, I'll buy you more fabric." He snatched up a dry towel and looped it over her shoulders. Then without letting go of the ends, tugged her closer.

Hair plastered on top of her head, she lifted a defiant gaze and waited.

Even with her long lashes glistening with water…

And raccoon eyes from running mascara…

Even though she glared at him like Sister Mary Margaret…

Jill was *the* most enchanting and adorable woman he'd ever met.

"You're so beautiful."

"I look like a drowned rat. A particular delicacy for eagles, I hear."

He glanced toward heaven and sighed.

"All right, you now have my attention." She huffed out an exasperated breath. "What do you want to say?"

"This." He released the towel and pulled her into his arms. His lips pressed against hers, then gently covered her mouth. Slow and thoughtful, with every intention of revealing his feelings for her, he allowed his kiss to linger and took it as a good sign when she didn't push him away. He lifted his head and gazed into her eyes. Thankful their rebellious glint had been replaced by a mixture of surprise and uncertainty.

He placed his fingers to her mouth. "Hold on to that. There's a promise behind it. I can't explain further, until I take care of one more little thing." Without taking his eyes off her, he asked, "Do you have anything to change into?"

"Yes."

"Promise me you won't leave town or do anything crazy, okay?"

She pulled the towel tightly over her shoulders. "Now you're just sounding like my mother." Jill spun away and marched from the bathroom.

* * *

It was well past midnight when Cam got back to his place. After he changed out of his wet clothes, he turned on the gas logs, then fixed himself a drink. He sat down in the leather wing chair nearest the fire determined to do some damage control of his own.

How in the world had he gotten here? Of all the people he'd exposed through his articles, what were the odds he'd end up blasting the woman he'd fallen in love with. As for Phil. The sooner he came clean about him the better.

He lifted a hand to his forehead. There had been so much more he'd wanted to say tonight. His kiss had been a placeholder of sorts, until he could figure out his next step. In light of all he'd done, he hoped it conveyed the truth that he cared deeply for her.

And the fact she hadn't pushed him away left him in little doubt as to her true feelings for him. At least that was something.

He spotted the red scarf Jill had given him at the bistro. That day, he'd come home, tossed it on the back of the sofa, with a mental note to never wear it around her as Cam.

But how to tell her about Phil, was the question now. The risk of her finding out through another source was unacceptable. If he expected to have any kind of a future with her, he'd have to confess everything. And soon.

He gripped the tumbler, eyeing the single cube of ice as he brought the glass rim to his lips. It would take more than clever words to write himself out of this one... Or would it?

Chapter Twenty-Five

Jill rarely slept in, but after her late night she hadn't woken up until noon. Truthfully, she was heartbroken. Everything she'd worked for would soon be history and worse, the man she'd fallen for was responsible.

She was never more grateful today was Sunday—a perfect day to hide from the *meanies* of the world. The plan? Hold up in Daniel Livingston's brownstone for the duration. If she'd had to get up for work she'd have been miserable. Sadly, her only task now was to pack it all in.

She pulled a thoroughly steeped teabag from her cup, then proceeded to spoon in a liberal amount of sugar.

It was nearing three o'clock and she hadn't heard another word from Cam since he'd left her office the previous night. She touched a finger to her mouth. His kiss had been surprisingly gentle and more persuasive than she cared to admit. His parting cryptic remark still perplexed her, and she had to confess to a growing curiosity as to what one thing he could be referring to.

She'd pretty much gotten used to the fact that Cameron and the Eagle Eye were one and the same. Seeing him in the audience during her speech while she blamed the Eagle for her situation was rather surreal. She'd wanted to protect Annie and it had been easy to blame the Eagle for her current situation. But maybe it hadn't been fair to blame him. After all, Cameron had only written what he'd seen.

In the light of day she felt a bit more rational. More inclined to see his side of things. Last night, he'd come after her. Tried to explain. Refused to leave her, even after her rant with the coffee stirrers. She smiled at the memory, then thought about her beautiful dress and frowned. Tipping the cup to her lips, she downed the rest of her tea.

Since the beginning, he'd known who she was and could have ended their relationship anytime. But he hadn't. He was charming and kind, and at times seemed to go out of his way to be with her. That could only mean one thing. He was truly interested in taking the next step. She pressed the side of her head onto the arm of the sofa and sighed.

There was a knock on her door. It was Amy. She held up the *New York Post*. "You are *not* going to believe it."

"Oh, no? What's happened now?"

"You need to read something." Close to giddy, Amy handed her the paper. "I've flagged the section for you."

After they both sat down, Jill opened to the part Amy had marked. A few minutes later she looked up.

"Well?" Amy's face glowed.

"It's very nice."

"I'll say. Why aren't you happy? It's an article about you. It's beautiful. It exonerates you. Cameron shows you as generous and kind with a heart for the disadvantaged. It's all about New Hope and the people you've worked with there. Things I didn't even know. And he's included your volunteer work with Annie's girls. An article like this could turn your business around. I thought you'd be pleased."

"I am. It's quite flattering, but at this point who's going to believe it? Or even see it?" She folded the newspaper and placed it on the coffee table. "The damage has already been done."

"But—"

"Fifty articles could be written espousing my many virtues, but they wouldn't make any difference. It has to come from the Eagle. And it never will."

"Maybe the Eagle will respond by writing a retraction after this."

"It's doubtful."

There was no way Cam would give up his anonymity over this and truthfully, she wouldn't want him to. His articles, including the one on the homeless, were excellent and the fact he pointed fingers made him audacious, daring, and risky. An appealing trait to his fans.

After last night, she knew he felt remorseful over the article. He'd actually looked devastated. Even his kiss had held a sense of desperation. She wondered if the one little thing he'd referred to had been this recent piece on her. His honest, affirming words touched her deeply. It was enough that she alone knew the man who'd once accused her, now exonerated her. Hope nudged her heart, bringing with it a sense of urgency. Maybe love did conquer all. He'd said he'd contact her. She'd just have to wait and see.

* * *

Cam turned to his article in the *Post*, wondering if Jill even knew about it. In it he'd talked about her work with Steve. Re-reading that section, it still moved him.

He picked up his cell and punched in Jill's number. It rang five times before she finally picked up.

"Hey, it's Cameron. I hope I didn't catch you at a bad time."

"No, this is fine."

"I wrote an article about you. It's in the *Post*."

"I know. Amy was just here. She brought me the newspaper."

"Good." He waited, hoping she'd say something more, but all he heard was silence. "You deserve an article like this. I felt it was the least I could do, considering..."

"Thank you. It was very nice. Really. But I doubt it'll turn things around."

He'd hoped her response would be different. Today's article put Jill in a positive light and if enough in her industry read it, she would be vindicated.

But hidden on page six, it was unlikely anyone who mattered would actually read it. It wasn't enough that Jill had seen it, her industry needed to read it as well.

She'd already lost so much because of him. The stigma—already in place.

"So, was this article the *other little thing* you mentioned?"

"Partly. Will you meet me for dinner at the Plaza tomorrow night? Say seven?"

He held his breath. *Please say yes.*

"If this means we can finish our conversation from the other night, then yes. I have to admit to being curious as to how you knew about Phil, among other things."

"Good. Seven then."

CHAPTER TWENTY-SIX

"Knock, knock!" A pleasant feminine voice called out from the main entrance.

Jill and Amy stopped packing boxes and stared at the attractive lady opening the entry door to JJ Designs.

"I hope I'm not disturbing you."

"Not at all," Jill said. "Please come in."

The lady crossed the room and handed Jill a business card. "I'm Jen Talbot, owner of Lilly Bette's boutiques."

"Oh, my gosh. I love your stores. I'm Jill Jeffrey and this is my assistant, Amy Stallings."

Jen smiled. "I know who you are and that's exactly why I'm here."

Jill glanced at Amy who stood wide-eyed, mirroring Jill's own internal amazement at their surprise guest.

"What can I do for you?"

"I see you're in the middle of something, so I'll get right to the point. I heard about what happened with Sloan's. As a public company I understand why they had to cancel, but that's not the case for me, or my retail business." She noticed the dress forms lined up along the far wall and walked over. "Are these the prototypes you did for them?"

"Yes."

Jen took a turn around each, inspecting the work. "The crop top paired with the denim overalls is adorable. I absolutely love what you've done here."

"I'm sorry," Jill said. "How did you know about my designs?"

"Sloan's buyer, Liz Fuller, is a friend of mine. She told me what I'd find here. Said I'd be crazy if I didn't secure your designs immediately. Unless you have another offer, consider it done."

"I...thank you." Jill's breath caught in her throat.

"After the holidays I want to see the rest of them. Say January third?"

"The third is fine."

"You've got my card. Email me between now and then and I'll send you the details."

"Okay."

When Jen reached the entrance, she glanced back. "And I'd stop all that packing if I were you." She smiled. "Merry Christmas." Jen closed the door behind her.

"Talk about blind-sided, but in a totally good way." Eyes still enormous, Amy touched a hand to her mouth.

"Ditto."

For a moment Jill and Amy gaped at each other.

"I'll start putting the bins back on the shelves." Amy patted Jill's shoulder. "And you? Put a smile on your face."

"I think I will." Jill glanced at the business card between her fingers. What the heck just happened?

* * *

Jill took great pains in deciding what to wear for her evening with Cam. This could end up being their last time together and she wanted to look amazing.

She wore her hair down and after taking her time with her makeup, she slipped on a sapphire blue taffeta dress. She'd made it a few weeks ago when she thought she'd be seeing more of Cam.

Things seemed to be turning around for her. Thanks to Jen at Lilly Bette's, she and Amy were still in business. As wonderful as that news had been, it was not enough to ease the pain. At one time her work had brought her great joy, but no longer. Discovering Cam's dual identity had caused a major upheaval in her personal life. An inner turmoil that had yet to be resolved.

Discovering the man she'd fallen for was the same person who'd single-handedly wrecked her life and career had been unsettling. She had so many unanswered questions and needed answers if she was to heal and move on.

But did she really want to move on? Heal yes, but how could she heal if Cameron wasn't a part of her life? She pinched the bridge of her nose between her fingers. The whole thing was way too confusing. She'd just have to see how the evening played out.

As Jill pushed through the hotel doors, the glittering holiday décor greeted her in all of its sparkling extravagance. She entered the Plaza restaurant and approached the check-in desk. "I'm Jill Jeffrey dining with Cameron Phillips."

"Yes. Right this way." The Maître d' escorted her past the ornate columns to a private dining room. A single table for two sat invitingly in the center of the paneled room. The small centerpiece of gold and silver glowed in the soft light, creating a scene both romantic and intimate.

"Mr. Phillips just stepped out and will be back shortly. May I take your coat?"

"No, thanks. I'm still feeling a bit chilly."

"Very good. There's a hook beside the door for your convenience. Would you like something to drink while you wait?"

"No, I'm fine."

She remained standing after he left and perused the paintings in the room. There were three in total, all depicting iconic buildings in New York City. The one of the Brooklyn Bridge conjured up a longhaired, bearded Phil. An intense longing tugged her heart, bringing with it a feeling of failure and restlessness.

She gazed at the painting, wondering if he'd ever followed up with Spencer. The fact that she hadn't heard was a sure sign he had not. She'd failed Steve and now, it seemed, Phil. *Stubborn, stubborn man.*

Sufficiently warmed up, she removed her long coat and hung it on the hook next to Cam's cashmere. Odd. She'd never seen him wear it before. She ran her hand over the soft material and down the length of the coat. Same color as the one she'd given Phil over two months ago. She opened the lapel and, hanging inside along with the coat, was a red scarf. She fingered it. Alpaca wool. Her heart stopped. *It can't be.* She glanced at the upper inside pocket. The letters MB stared back at her. *Mark Billings.* Oh God. Cameron was Phil. And she'd hurt and humiliated him from the very beginning.

As her thoughts scrambled to understand, she closed her eyes and lifted the scarf to her face.

"Excuse me."

Cameron. He'd come back. Heart thudding, she opened her eyes and turned toward him.

* * *

Cam fixed his gaze on Jill's face and stepped slowly across the room. As he approached, her eyes pooled with unshed tears. When he reached her, he carefully lifted the scarf from her unresisting fingers, then placed it around his neck.

"I believe this is mine."

Her mouth parted as a single tear fell onto her cheek, then another.

"It's a special gift from a young woman who's very dear to me. Who finds joy in helping others, expecting nothing in return. I'd hate to lose it, or her."

Jill brushed at her tears and continued to stare at him. A mixture of disbelief and awe flowed from her eyes as she studied his features.

He took hold of her hands and clasped them to his chest. "In case you have a sudden impulse to run away."

She gave a quick shake of her head. "How is this possible?" Sniffing, she tugged one hand free and gently placed her palm to his cheek. "You look nothing like him."

"Very different. I know. I hardly recognized myself."

"I hurt you. I hurt you and I'm so sorry."

"You have nothing to apologize for." He gave a slight squeeze to her hands. "Besides, you already did."

"What do you mean?"

"In your speech the other night. What you said about Phil moved me deeply."

Clutching the lapels of his suit, she buried her face against his chest.

His arms encircled her and his heart soared. "Now you're making me wish I'd told you sooner."

She pushed out of his embrace. "There were a couple of times when you reminded me of him. A look, a turn of phrase, but I chalked it up to wishful thinking."

"Then you're not disappointed? You're not angry?"

"No. There were times when I so wanted it to be true."

"After my article, I thought I'd messed things up for sure. Let's sit down."

She took her seat as he pulled his chair to the side near hers. After he sat, he clasped one of her hands and faced her. He loved the way her eyes glowed at this very moment, devouring his features as if trying to see the resemblance.

"The day you walked into Annie's office…" He shook his head. "All I thought about was that blasted article. I rationalized —told myself I'd written the truth. That carried me along for a while, until I got to know you. Then it became clear I'd told *my* truth, but not necessarily *the* truth."

Smiling through her tears, she shook her head and gazed at him in wonder. "No matter. I'm just so happy to have found you." She squeezed his hand. "To know you're safe. And that tonight you'll have a good meal and a warm place to sleep."

"You do know you're talking to me—Cameron."

"I know. I know." She shook her head. "It's weird. *I'm* weird."

He laughed. "Then I love weird."

"I'm just thankful I don't have to worry about my street guy anymore."

"Your street guy."

"Yes, that's how I thought of Phil."

"I'll be your street guy anytime you want."

She placed her palms to each side of his face. "I just knew someone sexy and extremely appealing hid behind that disheveled look." Dreamy-eyed, she looped her arms around his neck.

"I'd be more than happy to accommodate you." Heart pounding, he feathered kisses along her jaw. "I'll stop shaving tomorrow."

"I was half in love with him, you know."

"I know. And just so *you* know, I had to stop Phil from kissing you at least twice."

She smiled, revealing her single, sweet dimple. Wanting to kiss that one spot more times than he could count, he did so now.

"Dearest Jill, I want to apologize for the pain I've caused you. I've never been more wrong about a person's motives than I was about yours."

"Thank you for that. The words hurt much more when I found out the man I'd fallen in love with had written them."

"Oh, sweetheart. Please forgive me." He stood and pulled her into his arms. "I want you to know, I'm fully prepared to reveal the Eagle's identity if things don't get better for you."

"No. No." She pushed slightly away and gazed up at him. "You can't do that. You were right about me, in part. And the last thing I want is for you to blow your cover. You're talented and articulate. I especially loved the piece on underage drinking. Your articles are brilliant. Not that I'm an expert. But you have a way of emotionally bringing the reader into the issue, while getting to the heart of the matter."

He cocked his head to the side. "Really?"

She nodded. "I know, because I've read every Eagle article to date. Granted, it started out with me trying to figure out who you were, but still."

"That's not an exceptional feat since there's only five."

Cam felt undeserving of the open admiration spilling from Jill's eyes. "And Eagle Eye's touch of venom?"

She scrunched up her nose. "Not my favorite part."

"You're in good company. My mother feels exactly the same way."

"I like your mother already."

He brushed his lips across her forehead. "Speaking of your street guy, I went to see Spencer."

She brightened.

"Not as Phil, of course. But to talk to him about employment for one of the homeless men I've come to know. Thanks to you, Eddie starts work in January."

"That's wonderful. I have good news, too. Do you remember that darling boutique I told you about, Lilly Bette's?"

"I do."

"Well, the owner found out what happened with Sloan's and wants my designs."

"Does that mean you're still in business?"

"It does. But you don't look too pleased."

"No, it's not that." He reached inside his suit jacket and pulled out a folded piece of paper. "It's this."

She took it from his hand.

"It says you're the new owner of a small building in Greenwich Village. I thought it might work as your first boutique."

"You did this?" Her voice held a note of surprise and gratitude.

"My mother actually. It seems she's a lot better at piddling than I thought."

"What?"

"I'll explain later when you two meet. But first…" He took her hands in his.

"Jillian Jeffrey. I've waited for you my whole life. You had me from the moment you handed me that coat. You take my breath away.

"Every.

"Time.

"I look at you."

Jill's eyes sparkled as she threw her arms around his neck. The scent of rose petals exploded around him—heady and wonderful. Holding her in this moment was all the joy he'd ever wanted.

"I love you, Jill." His lips slowly descended to meet hers. She melted against him, responding with a sweet abandon that touched his soul.

In the distance, the orchestra started playing, *Have I Told You Lately*.

"They're playing our song," she whispered against his lips.

He reluctantly put her away from him, pushed back his sleeve, and checked his watch. "And right on time."

She chuckled with that husky little laugh he'd come to love.

"Mr. Phillips, are you manipulating the circumstances?"

"Not at all. May I have this dance?"

"Yes." Glowing with all the joy of being in love, she stepped back into his arms.

EPILOGUE

Jill and Dorothy Phillips stood behind Cam's desk chair as he pondered the next word in his exposé´.

"You can't use that word," Dorothy said.

"Your mother's right. *Manipulative* is much too harsh."

He blew out a breath, hit delete, and typed in *scheming*.

"Nope. Can't use that one either," Jill said. "What about *calculating*?"

"Oh, I like that," Dorothy said. "To the point without being mean."

Cam sat back and folded his arms. "Maybe one of you would like to write this?"

"No, no. You're doing fine, sweetheart." Jill patted his shoulder. She'd never seen him this exasperated. "You're so close to finishing. I'm sure Dick will be pleased."

Cam slowly pushed back his chair, stood, and folded his arms. He glared at the two women in the room. "Both of you." He pointed an aggressive finger toward the door. "Out."

"I know that look." His mother scrunched her face. "First time I saw it he was four." Dorothy scooped up her Loui Vuitton handbag and headed toward the door. "Don't forget lunch at Gramercy Tavern. They have *the* most divine martinis."

"She doesn't drink, Mother."

"Noon tomorrow," Jill said. "Can't wait, Dottie."

"I love my mother, but this thing between you two is really starting to scare me." He sat back down.

Jill chuckled and took a seat in Cam's lap, then slid her arms around his neck. His gaze roamed her features, and her heart soared. She belonged to him. "Do I have to go, too?"

"I suppose my mother put you up to this." He nodded toward his current article. "I thought you'd come to respect my no-holds-barred jargon."

"I do. I just prefer you dip them in a bit of honey first." Jill fingered his beard. "This has grown out nicely." Between each word, she planted kisses on his neck, jaw, and face.

"You think?"

"Mmmm, yes. It's not every day a woman gets to be with the two men she loves most."

"You're irresistible and you know it. Is it any wonder I'm having trouble finishing this article?"

She chuckled against his cheek.

"Speaking of honey." His warm lips came coaxingly down on hers and she drank in the sweet nectar of his kiss.

A moment later, he lifted his head and gazed lovingly at her.

"I take it this means I can stay?" she said.

He wrapped his arms around her waist and tugged her closer. "You're incorrigible. And yes, as my fiancé you have a special, all-access pass when it comes to being near me."

"I so like hearing that."

He lowered his mouth to hers, thoughts of his latest exposé temporarily forgotten.

Other Books in This Series

Hawke's Nest – Like No Other Book 1

Running away is nothing new for Annie Dell, aka high-fashion model Anna Delany. With the paparazzi hot on her trail, an out of town wedding couldn't have come at a more opportune time. What better place to hide out than the quaint Florida beach town Liddy's told her so much about. But a delayed flight, mix up with the car rental, then a speeding ticket from the local *Sheriff of Nottingham*, her getaway is looking anything but relaxing.

Franklin County Sheriff, Levi Hawke, is tired of the spoiled, out-of-control students on fall break, who think they can speed through his county without consequence. After giving a ticket to a beautiful young woman he assumes is just another *daddy's* girl looking for some fun in the sun, he discovers she's his weekend date at his best friend's wedding.

Through gritted teeth, masked by a half-hearted truce, they survive the weekend, only to find themselves stranded alone in the middle of a hurricane. *You can discover a lot about a person while spending thirty-six hours without the comforts of electricity and modern conveniences.* When circumstances further extend her stay in town, Levi pries deeper to find out what Annie's running from. He knows when someone is haunted by their past. As the saying goes ... it takes one to know one.

Thank you for reading!

Dear Reader,

I hope you enjoyed **Eagle Eye: Like No Other Book 2**. If you're wondering how my Like No Other Series started, check out **Hawke's Nest: Like No Other Book 1**.

I need to ask a favor. As you probably know, reviews can be hard to come by. And as a reader your feedback is so important. If you're so inclined, I'd love an honest review of *Eagle Eye*. It doesn't have to be long or fancy. :) One or two sentences is fine.

If you have time, here's a link to my author page on Amazon. You can check out all my books here:

http://www.amazon.com/-/e/B0077AG3ZM

In gratitude,
Darcy Flynn

ABOUT THE AUTHOR

Darcy Flynn is known for her heartwarming, sweet contemporary romances. Her refreshing storylines, irritatingly handsome heroes and feisty heroines will delight and entertain you from the first page to the last. Miss Flynn's heroes and heroines have a tangible chemistry that is entertaining, humorous and competitive.

Darcy lives with her husband, son, two English Setters and a menagerie of other living creatures on her horse farm in Franklin, Tennessee. She raises rare breed chickens, stargazes on warm summer nights and indulges daily in afternoon tea.

Although, published in the Christian non-fiction market under her real name, Joy Griffin Dent, it was the empty nest that turned her to writing romantic fiction. Proving that it's never too late to follow your dreams.

Please follow Darcy on Twitter: https://twitter.com/darcy flynn and Facebook: http:/www.facebook.com/DarcyFlynn Author, and visit her website: http://www.darcyflynnromances .com/, or feel free to drop her a line at: darcyflynnromances@ gmail.com.

OTHER TITLES BY DARCY FLYNN:

CPSIA information can be obtained
at www.ICGtesting.com
Printed in the USA
LVHW022111060921
697100LV00004B/99

9 781941 925096